Arafat Is Next!

Arafat Is Next!

LIONEL BLACK

𝔰𝔡
STEIN AND DAY/Publishers/New York

First published in 1975
Copyright © 1975 by Lionel Black
All rights reserved
Designed by David Miller
Printed in the United States of America
Stein and Day/*Publishers*/Scarborough House,
Briarcliff Manor, N.Y. 10510

Library of Congress Cataloging in Publication Data

Black, Lionel
    Arafat is next!

    I. Title.
PZ3.B24234Ar3 [PR6003.A679]   823'.9'12   74-29318
ISBN 0-8128-1761-3

1

The dark, well-dressed, sharp-featured young man stood hesitant at the entrance to the office building. That Monday morning in August the hazed London sunshine was already warming the street; but not sufficiently to cause the trickles of sweat around his mouth, which the young man was touching nervously with a folded white handkerchief. His other hand was gripping the handle of a black leather briefcase so tautly that the skin over the knuckles was stretched white.

He gave a swift, almost desperate look along the street. Then he stepped quickly into the darkened entrance hall of the building and up one flight of stone stairs to the door bearing on its frosted glass the name of an Israeli export firm. Not hesitating now, he went swiftly in.

The small reception area was bounded by a mahogany barrier, beyond which sat three typists, one doubling on the telephone switchboard. The right-hand door behind them led into Mr. Katz's office, the left-hand door into the general office. It happened that Aaron Hirsch was just leaving Mr.

Katz's office to return to his own desk. Hirsch was regarded as a coming young man. A strictly Orthodox Jew and a fervent Zionist, he had emigrated four years earlier from New York to Israel, in time to serve with distinction in the June war. He then joined the export firm's head office in Tel Aviv, and at the end of 1969 was transferred to the London branch.

One of the girls looked up sharply, surprised by the abruptness of the visitor's entrance. But then she rose, smiling dutifully, to inquire his business.

The dark young man said nothing. For a moment he stood motionless. Then he threw his briefcase over the barrier onto the floor at the girl's feet, turned, and fled.

Hirsch did not hesitate. He stooped to grab the briefcase and ran swiftly from the office, down the stairs, into the street.

There were too many people around.

He sprinted for St. James's Square. He could lob the filthy thing over the railings into the square's garden and, with luck, nobody would be hurt.

He would have made it if he had not collided at the corner of the square with a man walking rapidly. Hirsch himself was going so fast that the collision jerked the briefcase from his hand. It fell into the gutter.

"Run," he shouted at the astonished stranger. "Run. It's a bomb."

Hirsch stooped to get it from the gutter. He had his hand on it when it exploded.

By a freak of the explosion he lost his right hand—a tatter of flesh, small broken bones, and blood dangling from his wrist—but not his life.

The other man was killed instantly. His body, almost severed at the waist, lay athwart the gutter, an incongruous mess of blood and guts in a formal dark suit. His hard hat bowled across the roadway. His rolled umbrella was twisted into a tangle beneath him.

Police and ambulances were there in minutes. Aaron Hirsch was sped to Charing Cross Hospital. The other man, laid out in the second ambulance, was taken to the Westminster morgue. Before the body was removed, the police found from his breast-pocket wallet that the man's name was Anthony Dunton. The wallet held several credit cards and an entry pass for the Ministry of Defence. He had been on his way, they later ascertained, to a lunch appointment with his twin brother, for which he was already a little late, at his club in Pall Mall.

That night, over radio from Damascus, a Palestinian terrorist group claimed the murder. They often lied, but this time they were probably telling the truth.

2

There were television and newspaper cameramen, Harvey Kennard noted warily, at the entrance porch of the village church in which Anthony Dunton's funeral was to take place. That could be dangerous. But nobody photographed him as he entered the church and found an unobtrusive pew.

The church was about half full, mostly of villagers. Kennard recognized a couple of Special Branch men. Yet he could see no reason for official surveillance. Dunton's death had been accident, mere chance.

Kennard himself was there because, for the sake of the family, someone from the department had to attend, and he had been closest to Dunton. Not that he was very close. Dunton had been a pleasant man, but never companionable. He had come into the service from a university career and had the reserve of an academic; but a good man at his job, particularly as a linguist. Not many Englishmen can pass as a Frenchman in France, a German in Germany, and almost any nationality of choice in the half dozen other countries in whose tongue he was fluent, but not sufficiently adept to pose as native.

The stained window above his pew, Kennard noticed, had been erected by the widow of Major General Archibald Dunton, who had gone to his rest in 1842. A wall plaque in the Lady chapel also bore the name of Dunton, as did the next stained window. From his pew Kennard made out one of the dates as 1730. The Duntons must have dominated the village for centuries. Kennard smiled at the Englishness of it. The Kennards came from one of the grubbier districts of Birmingham and he doubted if they could be traced back more than a couple of generations.

The coffin was borne in, followed by the family mourners—two men, three women, and three children. The men were black-haired and dark, the elder thick-shouldered and giving an impression of surly strength, the younger of slight build. Anthony Dunton had been black-haired and swarthy too. Once at the bar of the staff club in the basement of the department building, he had smilingly told Kennard that the family had been known locally in the eighteenth century as the Black Duntons.

One of the women was Jean Dunton, Anthony's widow. Kennard had met her twice at the stiff, formal parties she gave on New Year's at their home in a Surrey village near Guildford. The children were hers. The two other women must be the wives of the two brothers who now stood with them in the front pew.

After the graveside ceremony, as people were turning away, Jean Dunton came over to him. He murmured the usual awkward condolences.

"Thank you, Mr. Kennard," she said, "and thank you for being here. I hope you'll come back to the house."

"Of course," he agreed, slightly embarrassed, but curious.

It was a long, two-storied house of gray Purbeck stone, reached by a quarter-mile private drive from the village street. Behind it stood farm buildings.

The stone walls of the room in which a couple of dozen people gathered were hung with somber portraits, ancient swords, sabers, pistols, sporting guns. Most of the portraits were of men in military uniform stretching back for several centuries; all the men dark, recognizably Duntons, most of them with the hard features and thin, prominent nose reproduced in the elder brother to whom Jean Dunton now introduced him. "Giles, this is Harvey Kennard, one of Anthony's colleagues, and a friend."

"Good of you to come, Mr. Kennard."

He had a deep, harsh voice, slightly touched with the Dorset burr. By his age, this brother must be Anthony's twin. Dissimilar, though. Seeing him close confirmed Kennard's impression of the man in the church—sullen, powerful, even brutal. Anthony, for all his courage, had been a gentle, quiet man.

"If there's anything the department can do . . . " Kennard said.

"There's nothing that any department can do. This is not a matter for a department."

Decanters of sherry and plates of sandwiches were set out on the long oak refectory table. Kennard took a glass and munched a ham sandwich, looking around him with curiosity—an old military family, planted like an oak in the English countryside, soldiering in all its country's wars but never otherwise distinguished; arrogant, silent men, curt toward women. Around the house, no doubt, stretched the fields which the family farmed in the intervals between wars. Kennard smiled thinly. The sword and the plowshare, but never the one beaten into the other. While the plow worked the fields, the sword hung on the wall, always ready for service.

He glanced across the room at the younger brother,

talking to the parson and two other men. He too had a neat, soldierly bearing but was in fact, Kennard vaguely recalled, a banker.

The guests were leaving. He asked Jean Dunton how he could get a taxi to Dorchester, to catch the next train to London. She phoned the village garage.

In the train Kennard ordered a large scotch from the restaurant-car waiter and sipped it gratefully. It was ridiculous, but he could not rid himself of a nagging uneasiness. He felt that there was something—but he knew not what—that he was trying to recall. He told himself irritably that it was simply that he always found funerals depressing, and that one had been grim.

3

That night of the funeral, when the meal was cleared, and the children had been sent to bed, the women to the drawing room, Giles Dunton summoned his brother to move up to his right at the head of the dining table. Giles fetched a decanter of port from the massive sideboard, filled his own glass, and pushed the decanter toward Mark.

"We must talk," he said somberly.

Mark glanced inquiringly, then understood. He filled his glass and asked, "Talk? About Anthony?"

"Yes, about Anthony."

As he said it, the pain Giles had striven to crush surged again. His fingers twisted on the stem of the glass so that some of the wine spilled on the dark oak of the table. Anthony was killed. Anthony!

The surge of pain was so strong that his head throbbed. He rose from his chair and walked to the window, staring into the dusk. It was not merely the closeness of twins. They were not identical twins and could scarcely have been more unlike, physically and mentally, if a few years had separated their births instead of a few hours. Anthony had none of the sullen strength of a typical Dunton. He grew from a delicate child into a frail adult with a tall, thinly fleshed frame, doubtful lungs, bronchial ills—and an indomitable spirit. The only man Giles ever revered; the only person in all his life whom he had loved.

Giles turned back from the window. "You scarcely knew him—really knew him."

"You two were so close, and I so much younger . . . "

Giles resumed his seat and reached for the decanter. "The bravest of the brave," he muttered.

"You mean in the war? Yes. The undercover outfit, and then pulled out of a concentration camp, when we overran it at the end, nearly dead."

"Belsen." Giles stared into his younger brother's eyes. "I had an average tough war. I took a tank across the Western Desert, through Tunisia, across to Sicily, and on the long slog up Italy. But I tell you this, Mark. My war was nothing compared to Anthony's."

He was silent for a while, gazing at his glass as he turned it slowly in his fingers.

"He wouldn't say much about it, even to me. After the army turned him down medically, he found a unit that needed languages—perfect French and German, from his schooling in Switzerland. He was parachuted into Europe, of course, time after time. In the end some bastard betrayed him. He was tortured. He wouldn't talk about it, but I'm certain he didn't break. Then he was cattle-trucked to the concentration camp."

Mark sat in silence. All this, of course, he already knew, but he understood Giles's need to say it.

Giles pushed the decanter toward him.

"And still it wasn't enough. After the war, when he went

up to Oxford on a late course, got his first, and a fellowship of his college, he could have spent the rest of his life there. But somebody from a back-door department in Whitehall told him he was needed again. Partly for his languages, I suppose. Mostly for his courage. There were long periods— did you know?—when even Jean had no idea where he was or what he was doing. I can guess. And that's the man who has been killed by some bloody Palestinian terrorist with a bomb."

Giles looked steadily across the table at his brother.

"They must pay."

"Pay? You mean retribution, revenge? But how? Britain isn't going to war with Jordan over an assassination." Mark allowed himself a cautious smile. "The days of the gunboat are past." He paused. "Giles, you're not serious?"

"Serious."

Mark refilled his glass and pushed the decanter toward Giles. "Tell me."

"An eye for an eye."

Mark stared at him, puzzled. "Even if we could find the bastard who carried the bomb, what'd be the use? We'd turn him over to the police. Within days, some of his chums would hijack an aircraft and threaten hostages until he was released and flown out to Cairo or Benghazi." He paused again, uncertain. "You mean we don't hand him over to the police? But it's not practical. To start with, how in hell do we find him?"

"Not him," answered Giles slowly. "He's only the courier. The way to stop this bloody campaign is to make the bastards understand that violence isn't always one-sided—by killing the man who orders it."

"You mean, just the two of us?"

"That's what I mean."

"We're to set out to get—who?"

"The man leading the Palestinians."

"Arafat? You mean Yassir Arafat? But he's not the wild man."

"He's their leader."

"Listen, Giles. I've been in that part of the world much more recently than you. In Aden I got to know a lot about Arab revolutionaries. Arafat isn't one. He's an educated man, a warped idealist, austere, implacable. He'll go on fighting the Israelis until they're forced out of Palestine—which will be never, of course. He won't last long anyway. There have been several attempts on his life. Only the other day Jordanian officers shot up a helicopter bringing him down somewhere, but although they hit the pilot, he landed the thing before he died, and Arafat got away with it."

"He won't get away from me."

Mark rose. "This is nonsense. Let's go to the women."

Giles gripped his arm. "I want your answer. Are you with me—or do I go alone?"

"But I tell you Arafat's the only reasonable man they've got. He's not behind the terrorism. He tries to curb it. When he goes, chances are the wild men will take over."

Giles released his brother's arm and leaned back in his chair.

"That has nothing to do with it. He's the Palestinians' leader. There are two good reasons why he's our man."

"Well?"

"So long as they're not stopped, the crazy men will go on roaming round Europe with bombs and Russian machine guns. The way to stop them is to reply in kind. Governments can't do that. But if one of their leaders were killed every time as reprisal, they'd soon be stopped. If they're not, hundreds more innocent people will be bombed or machine-gunned—like Anthony."

"The second reason is Anthony?"

"For me," said Giles harshly, "*the* reason."

Now it was Mark who turned away to the window, staring into the dark. Giles knew what was checking him. Not fear. Mark had done his military stint honorably, before handing in his commission to join the City merchant bank to which the youngest Dunton sons had always gone. Certainly not fear. It was his wife. Giles had scant opinion of Helen—pale blond prettiness, fake intellectual pretensions, fiddling about with books in a publishing house, refusing to have children because of what she called her career. And Mark infatuated, weakly giving in. Giles frowned. Weakness about women was not a trait with which he sympathized.

From the window Mark asked, "How long would it take?"

"At least a month."

After a pause, Mark said, "I suppose we might get close enough for a sniping shot."

Giles shook his head. "That wouldn't do. We have to get right up to him. We have to be sure."

"But how? Good God, Giles, there are a hundred obstacles. How do we get the weapons, how do we get them into Jordan? Arafat is always surrounded by a bunch of gunmen. Do you truly think the two of us could get that close, with a reasonable chance of getting away again?"

"I think so," answered Giles, softly now. "We're both trained soldiers with special qualification for this particular job. So far they've only been up against their own kind, usually in an atmosphere of hysteria. With careful planning, and the bit of luck every military operation needs . . ."

"You already have a plan?"

"So far, only a few ideas. I don't yet know whether there are to be two of us."

Mark did not reply.

"They killed Anthony," said Giles, still softly, but now viciously. "Do I go alone, or are you with me—yes or no?"

Mark turned suddenly. "It's yes, of course."

Giles rose without comment, making for the door.

"I'm going to London next Thursday. Meet me for dinner at my club the following Monday. We'll talk of ways and methods—if you really mean it."

"I've said so, haven't I? Of course I mean it."

"No reservations? No holding back?"

Mark slowly shook his head. "No holding back."

§

For two days Giles brooded. Once it was done, he and Mark must be able to step back into their normal lives. So each needed a cover story to account for his absence. For Mark that was easy; a business journey to the Arab states. For him, trickier; how account for a farmer leaving his farm as harvest started?

He began to establish his story on Sunday morning when Gwen came home from church. From his study window he watched her easing herself stiffly from her little car; like an old woman, though she was not yet fifty. That was what had become of the lively, spirited girl he had married twenty-four years ago. They had first met at an officers' dance in Jerusalem in 1946, when he had been posted to work with the Palestine Police during the Irgun troubles. Gwen had driven over with a party of friends from Beirut, where her father was a professor at the American University. Despite the sniping and bombing in Palestine, Giles still remembered that mood of joyful relief that the World War had ended. He had persuaded her to stay on by herself in Jerusalem. Within a week he had her in bed. Within a month they were married. They flew to Kenya for their honeymoon. He had been happy. It might even have lasted, he thought, had it not been for Elizabeth.

When Gwen was in, he went through to the drawing room, watching her lower herself awkwardly into a chair.

"Backache bad?"

She looked up, surprised at his solicitude. "It has been a little troublesome lately."

Neither pursued that; everything had been said years before. He had wanted a son. Their first child was Elizabeth. After a searing birth, Gwen had been warned of the medical risks of a second, and had had herself mutilated surgically without his knowledge. From that came the weakness of her body, and the far worse canker of hypochondria.

"I'm going away for a few weeks," he told her. "Anthony's death has shaken me more than I thought possible. I'm going away to—well, to get over it."

"Where will you go?"

"I haven't thought. I'll just wander off, probably somewhere abroad. How about you meanwhile?"

"Me?"

"I thought you might like to go to your mother. You would see Elizabeth."

For a moment she seemed too astonished to speak. Then he saw the fear creeping into her eyes that he was merely tormenting her.

"I mean it," he said.

At that she was pathetically grateful. "Oh, Giles, I would love it. Darling, I would love it."

He almost felt sorry for the poor bitch. It was years since she had called him darling. Had she missed the girl so much? Two years before, after one of their flaring rows, Elizabeth had gone off to her grandmother in America, then taken a job as children's nanny in an American family in nearby Boston, and written to tell him she would never return to England so long as he lived.

"We can shut the house," he said, "and leave the harvest to the bailiff. I'll buy your air tickets and arrange a letter of credit for five hundred dollars. You won't need more, staying with your mother."

The old woman, now widowed, and rich, would try to prevent Gwen from returning, he knew that. She had always hated him, and tried several times to lure Gwen away. He would deal with that, he grimly promised himself, when he got back.

As he turned to leave, he saw, with indifference, that she was quietly weeping. Not that she often wept.

A couple of days later he completed his cover story. He waited until dark before driving into Dorchester, more from convention than from any desire for secrecy. Several people knew that he was keeping a girl in that little boutique in a side street. Gwen surely knew, just as she must know that he went to London from time to time for women. She did not seem to care. If she privately cared, what of it? It was not true, as Elizabeth had screamed before she went, that Giles ill-treated his wife. He had not used her as a wife for years, but that was not ill treatment; on that score she was relieved. And she was secure in her position as his wife. He would never tolerate the humiliation of a divorce.

When he had parked his car, he walked around to the narrow courtyard at the rear of the boutique. There was light through the curtains of the upper window. Giles crossed the courtyard, took out his key, and opened the back door—then paused. From upstairs came sounds, laughter, little suppressed squeals. Giles tautened his lips, moved quietly up the stairs, eased open the door of the room.

The couple were on the bed, she on her back with her arms around his neck, he about to climb on top of her.

Giles took two swift steps, seized the man's ankles, twisted him onto the floor, cracking his head against the wall. The girl flinched back, groping for a bedcover. The man, red with rage and frustration, struggled up and came for him. Giles chopped him across the throat, then the neck; kicked him hard in the crotch. As the man doubled in pain, falling back on the floor, Giles twisted his arm behind him, hauled him to his knees, punched a fist into his face, then thrust him through the door and tumbled him down the stairs, running after, jumping on him with both feet in his back.

The man was groaning now, no longer yelling, only half conscious. Giles pulled open the door, lifted him to his feet and shoved him naked, sprawling, into the courtyard. Then he quietly shut the door, went upstairs, pitched the man's clothes out through the window to fall on him where he lay. Giles knew who he was, a fellow who kept a grocery store around the corner. He'd get his clothes on somehow, and crawl home. Giles shut the window and turned into the room.

The girl was crouched on the bed, terrified. "You've killed him."

"No, Sandra, he's not dead. I think he may have a broken nose, but I don't suppose he'll tell his wife how he got it."

She was looking up at him in fear, but yet with surges of frustrated desire; there was a streak across her chin where saliva had slipped from one corner of her mouth.

Giles smiled. Suddenly he found it amusing. That she

should have been thus aroused, and at the very moment deprived, pleased him.

He stared at her for a long minute, saying nothing. She watched him, still frightened, but confused, not knowing what he would do.

From his pocket he took a roll of notes and dropped them on the table.

"There's a hundred pounds there," he told her. "I'm going away for a month or so. You must manage on that, and anything you make from the shop, until I get back. If you run up bills you can't meet, I shall refuse to pay them, and throw you out. Clear?"

"Yes, Giles."

There was greed in her eyes now, and curiosity; but still covert fear, and bewilderment that he said nothing of what had happened. He noticed with amusement that she had let slip the bedcover to show one breast.

"You're going away?" she asked defensively. "Where are you going?"

"I don't know. Somewhere abroad. My brother's death has knocked me badly. I'm going away for a while."

Not that she gave a damn, he knew, about Anthony's death, or the effect it had on him. But he was making sure that any possible inquirer must find that everybody in his normal life knew he was away traveling, to get over the shock of Anthony. Giles believed in meticulous planning of an operation. No loose ends.

Suddenly he leaned across the bed, took hold of her jaw, and twisted her face up toward his; terror in her eyes again.

"So long as I keep you," he said softly, "you'd better not try it again with another man. If ever I find that you have, it won't end this way. Understand?"

She nodded, her tongue nervously wetting her lips.

He released her and stood up, then turned abruptly and went down out of the place, not looking back at her.

Driving home, he wondered to himself whether he had frightened her enough. He doubted it. For some time he had suspected that she was cheating. It was improbable that, once she had regained courage, she would now refrain. He ought to drop her, throw her out. But she had a flat belly, wonderfully firm breasts, and buttocks that more than filled a two-palmed grip; and he had never known even an expensive London whore with as delightful a skill as Sandra in titillation and then fulfillment.

§

When he had put his bag into the room he had reserved for a few nights in his club in St. James's, Giles went down to the bar, got himself a beer, and asked the barman whether the secretary was in the club.

"I think he's in the office, sir."

"Thanks. By the way, has Major Oliphant been into the club lately?"

"No sir, I haven't seen Major Oliphant for weeks. I think he's abroad."

Giles looked into the secretary's office. "Good morning, Harry. Do you happen to know where Bruce Oliphant is?"

"Sorry. I haven't seen him for some time, and I don't think we've a forwarding address for mail." He looked across at the clerk, who shook her head. "Arthur may know," he suggested.

"Of course. I'll ask him."

Arthur, who had been the club porter for three decades, never forgot anything he ever knew about every member;

and every member knew Arthur, though few could have given his surname. Arthur was standing, as usual, in his glass-and-mahogany box inside the entrance door. At Giles's question he hesitated. "I don't know for certain, sir, except that Major Oliphant is abroad. As to his exact whereabouts, probably the only gentleman who could tell you is Colonel Hawthorn. The colonel's in the club now, sir. He has just gone down to the bar."

Hawthorn was not a member whom Giles knew well; but Hawthorn would know that he and Oliphant were old colleagues and friends. Hawthorn was in the bar and, fortunately, standing by himself at one end.

"Giles Dunton," said Giles at the other's look of nonrecognition.

"Of course. Forgive me. It's a long time since we met. Damn sorry about your brother. A dastardly thing."

Giles nodded. "Thank you."

As the senior officer, Hawthorn asked what Dunton would drink, and bought him a beer.

"I need some information rather urgently," said Giles. "How can I get in touch with Bruce Oliphant?"

The sudden questioning look that Hawthorn gave him was sufficient giveaway. And it recalled to Giles something Bruce Oliphant had once hinted about Hawthorn.

"I take it," Giles said, "that he's in Ulster."

"He may be," answered Hawthorn coolly, noncommittal.

"I need very much to talk to him."

"Why?"

"You could say, because of what happened to my brother."

It was evident that Hawthorn understood. But he remained silent for some time. Giles guessed he was calculating how far he could be trusted. Suddenly the colonel made up his mind, took a letter from his pocket, tore a scrap off the envelope, wrote on it with his gold pencil, folded it, and handed it to Giles. "I guarantee nothing, but that might help."

"Thanks," said Giles, putting the paper away without looking at it.

"And now," continued Hawthorn, "you must forgive me. I am expecting a luncheon guest upstairs."

§

Not until he was back in his bedroom did Giles take the torn piece of envelope from his pocket. On it Hawthorn had written, in his trim, small hand, a Belfast telephone number and a name, Sam B. Giles memorized the number, then put a light to the piece of paper and let it burn out in the ashtray beside his bed. He emptied the ashes out of the window and they dispersed in the slight summer breeze.

From the central London section of the classified telephone directory below the bedside table he picked out two small travel agencies, both in side streets, one in Mayfair, the other in Knightsbridge.

At the Mayfair office he bought Gwen's air tickets to and from Boston, telling the travel agent that his wife was to visit her mother in America. For business reasons he could not accompany her. He wanted her taken care of from the moment she left the house in Dorset until she arrived at her mother's home near Boston. The travel agent assured him there was no problem except the entry visa. Since time was short, Mrs. Dunton must visit the embassy in Grosvenor Square in person. Giles instructed him to see to it.

Next morning he took a No. 9 bus to Knightsbridge. A

taxi ride might be identified, but nobody could trace a bus journey. There was a woman working alone in the travel office, and he found her intelligent and efficient. He told her he was seeking a Mediterranean cruise holiday during the next few weeks. She handed him brochure after brochure, each one of which he quickly scanned, then passed back; not quite what he was looking for. He had cousins in Beirut and hoped to get ashore to visit them. None of the cruises in the brochures put in at Beirut.

"Is that really all there is?" he asked.

She paused, tapped her teeth absently with the butt of her pencil. She had regular, very white teeth. Suddenly she pointed the pencil at him. "Wait a minute, sir. There's a small French line that starts from Marseilles, and I think. . . ."

She was searching through typed sheets at the back of a filing cabinet, and at last emerged with one.

"Yes," she triumphed, "there's a call at Beirut. The next sailing, from Marseilles, is Friday, August 28."

"And can I spend a day ashore?"

"Of course. It's even better. If you want to see something of the Lebanon, there's an arrangement by which you can leave the ship at Beirut and catch it up by air, rejoining it either at Alexandria or Tunis, the two next ports of call."

"How long would that give me in Lebanon?"

"Let's see. The ship gets to Alexandria two days after leaving Beirut, and Tunis four days after that. If you took the longer break you would have five clear days in Lebanon."

Giles laughed. "And how much of that ancient country could one hope to see in five days?"

She was excited. "They've thought of that too, sir. Lots of passengers must have said the same—or perhaps it's the old French connection with Lebanon. You can leave the cruise at Beirut, then rejoin the line's next cruise at the same port a month later. I think the fare's the same. No, there's a small surcharge but only a thousand francs."

"I'll think about it. But book me on the August 28 sailing. I suppose you haven't got a cabin plan."

"Afraid not. But I can get one by tomorrow. The line has agents in London. Where can I call you?"

"I'll come in," he said. "My name's Dunton. I'll bring my passport and everything else necessary tomorrow. Shall I leave you a deposit?"

"Say ten pounds?"

He put a couple of notes on her desk. "I shall want to pick up the tickets as soon as possible. Can it be on Monday?"

"Your check would have to go through," she demurred.

"I'll go to my bank and bring cash. Roughly how much?"

She consulted another paper. "This is last year's list, but it can't have risen by more than 50 percent. It says here £140 for a cabin on A deck. I don't think it could be much more than two hundred. A deck sounds rather grander than it is, sir. It's not one of the large lines, and the ship is only four thousand tons. But I booked a passenger and his wife last summer and they were very satisfied. They said the food was super."

"If I bring three hundred in cash, in case you have underestimated, can you issue me the ticket on Monday?"

"I'm sure I can, sir," she agreed, smiling. She had really the most seductive smile, such beautifully regular teeth.

§

By the time his brother arrived for dinner on Monday, Giles had the steamer tickets in his holdall in his bedroom. He had opted for the month's break at Beirut.

Giles got a table in the far corner of the huge dining room so he and Mark would not be overheard. When the food was served, Mark asked, "Well, what's the plan?"

"For you, a preliminary mission. My car's in the usual garage off Berkeley Square. Here are the keys, and the garage ticket. I need to have the car in Paris by tomorrow week—that's Tuesday the twenty-fifth—in the garage attached to the Hôtel Mercurieur; I've marked the position on this Paris street map. I have a room booked there and they've been told my car is coming over from England. We mustn't meet."

"I'll visit the bank's Paris office. I quite often do."

"Make the car ferry booking as soon as you can. The ferries are crowded in August. You must fly back to London, because you must be booked on a flight to Bahrain next day. Can there be a plausible reason for that?"

Mark nodded. "I'll tell the bank I've a contact there—and in fact I have—who can swing some investment of oil funds in our direction. We already handle a lot from the Trucial States."

"But you don't go to Bahrain," Giles continued. "Get off at Beirut. Don't tell anybody you're breaking the journey until you're actually airborne from London. Get a Lebanon visa before you start. Can the break at Beirut be plausible too?"

"Yes. We've several banking connections there. I can have heard something from a fellow passenger which would suggest an advantageous stop."

"Good. But hold that in reserve. Don't bring it out unless you have to. Don't send word back to London. Put up at one of the smaller hotels in Beirut. Make one or two contacts— people you already know, for preference. Say you've decided on a short vacation. Hire a self-drive car and talk about an excursion round the mountains in the north, and a possible trip to Damascus. I plan to arrive in Beirut on September 2—that's the following Wednesday. Leave word at the American Express where I can contact you. We'll take it from there when I telephone you, probably on that day."

All either of them wanted after meat was a slice of Stilton and a glass of port. When that was served, Mark said, "It's going to be more difficult than you know. I've been talking to one or two of our Middle East experts."

Giles looked at the next table, where a couple of men he knew were settling.

"Finish the cheese, and let's go to the library for coffee," he said. "It'll be quiet there."

As indeed it was; only two members reading at tables by the window, and one snoozing in an armchair. Giles led to a couple of chairs at the distant end and, when their coffee had been brought by a waiter of elderly decrepitude, said, "Well?"

"It's Arafat himself. He's going to be that much more difficult to get at, because he has unquestioning loyalty from his followers. He's always surrounded by men who revere him and would die to protect him. It's because he's single-minded, and has no ideologies, no theories, just a determination to force the Israelis into the sea and get Palestine back for the Palestinians. They understand that. He doesn't bother them with wild theories, like the other would-be leaders, most of them Marxist or Maoist. And he's fanatically austere, scorns comfort, lies down to sleep on the floor wherever he is at night, probably in a corner of some filthy refugee hut. There's a story that he had one of his men whipped for serving him coffee in a china cup when his lieutenants were drinking out of tin mugs."

Giles stared at him. "Are you weakening?"

Mark flushed. "You know I'm not. You have my word—no reservations. But obviously the more we know about the man the better."

Giles assented, without much interest.

"We're going to need to plan every detail," Mark insisted.

"Of course."

"Weapons, for instance. Timetable for the operation. Where we're to go, how we can get close enough—and whether it's possible to get close, or should we depend on sniping rifles."

"Close," said Giles. "That's sure. As for the rest, that must come later. Just make the moves, on the days I've named, and when we meet in Lebanon we can plan what follows."

Mark reluctantly agreed. After hesitation he added, "There's one personal thing. I have a bank loan on the security of my house in Fulham—not from our bank, but on an ordinary loan account with Lloyds, where Helen and I have our joint account for day-to-day living."

"Well?"

"I don't want even a slight risk of leaving Helen with that liability. She'd have to sell the house. Will the estate lend me enough to pay it off temporarily—repayable to the estate when we get home?"

"How much?"

"Around two thousand pounds."

"All right. Send details to the lawyer. I'll scribble a note to him before I go to bed. Now let's go down to the bar for a nightcap, then I'll ask you to go home. I've a tough time ahead. I need sleep tonight."

§

When he came down in the morning, carrying his grip, Giles stopped the porter getting him a taxi. Instead he walked up to Piccadilly and took the untraceable underground from Green Park station to Hounslow; thence the airport shuttle bus to Heathrow.

He had made no advance booking; plenty of aircraft to Belfast. He bought a tourist single to Aldergrove. When the girl asked for his luggage, he answered shortly that he had only one small grip which he would take into the cabin with him. For the passenger list he gave a false name—undetectable, since no passport was required.

The aircraft was not full. Several of the passengers were obviously army officers in mufti, returning from leave. Three or four of the others, he fancied, were policemen. Giles took a seat near the tail of the aircraft. The seat beside him was unoccupied.

At Aldergrove he found a telephone booth to dial the number Colonel Hawthorn had given him.

The Irish voice at the other end said simply, "Hello."

"I'd like to speak to Sam B."

"Who is it?"

"My name is Dunton. You won't know me."

"Oh, yes, we know you, Major Dunton. Where are you?"

"I'm at Aldergrove in the front hall."

"What would you be wearing?"

"Tweed jacket, gray slacks, brown shirt, brown woolen necktie, no hat. I'm carrying a small grip."

"There are padded seats by the wall near the phone booth. Buy an English newspaper and sit in one of those seats, reading it, with the grip at your feet. Wait until somebody comes and says he is Sam B. Then do as he tells you."

"Very well."

"Has anybody followed you?"

"I'm sure not."

"If you think you're being watched, tell Sam B. that you don't know him, and you're waiting for your wife. He'll make off. Wait a quarter of an hour, then dial this number again."

"I'm sure it won't be necessary."

"Never be sure of anything in Ulster, Major."

The phone went dead.

Giles went to the nearest newspaper kiosk, bought *The Times,* and settled in the middle seat of the row. From time to time he looked casually around, certain at first that nobody was paying attention to him, but later not so sure. A small man in a raincoat was hanging about near the kiosk, looking at the magazine racks. Once or twice, glancing up from his newspaper, Giles found this man looking in his direction; but not necessarily at him. It was slightly worrying.

The people using the seats were continually changing. Giles expected Sam B., when he arrived, to sit by him, pretending not to know him at first. But after nearly half an hour a tall, grizzled man in slacks and open-neck shirt walked straight toward him. Giles glanced once more at the little man in the raincoat, who was still standing by the kiosk, but not looking in his direction. It was just somebody waiting, Giles decided. Nobody could have followed his trail from London, or had any idea where he might have taken himself; and why should anybody?

So when the tall man came up to him, hand extended, he rose and took it.

"I'm Sam B. I've a car outside."

"Fine," said Giles, picking up his grip and following.

The car was an elderly Morris. The grizzled man drove first toward Belfast center, then turned into a suburban maze. Giles, unfamiliar with the city, soon had no idea where he was or in which direction he had come. When he spoke to the driver, he got only monosyllables, so he fell silent.

In a poor, narrow street the car turned suddenly into the back yard of a small public house. The driver led the way through a rear door, upstairs to a bedroom overlooking the yard.

"I'm to leave you here."

"Somebody will soon be coming?"

"Oh, sure. Just a few inquiries to be made first, they were telling me."

The man backed through the bedroom door. As he closed it, Giles heard the key turn in the lock. He resisted the impulse to walk over and try the door. Instead he sat in a rickety armchair that stood by the window and resigned himself to waiting.

4

Harvey Kennard boiled himself an egg for breakfast and took a cup of tea to Sally, who was still in bed, her blond hair twisted into curlers and her face slightly greasy with overnight cream. He stooped to kiss her. She returned the kiss coldly. They both knew why, but she had not talked of it, and he was not going to be the first to bring it into the open. So he smiled cheerfully and went to his breakfast. He called to her as he left, walking sharply toward the station.

He disliked commuting and sometimes sadly recalled the smart apartment they had rented in Chelsea, before the succession of hard knocks that had compelled him to cut expenses, try to mend his emotional hurts, and move to a top-floor walkup in the shabby, characterless suburb of Herne Hill, grateful for the security of an underpaid government job.

The electric train was crammed, but the journey to Charing Cross brief, and thence it was only a short walk to the department's small unobtrusive door in the rear of a Whitehall building.

There was a note on his desk that Captain Carter had phoned. He dialed the extension. "Hello, Jim. Harvey Kennard. Is it all right?"

"You'd better come down here."

Kennard crossed the bridge into the main building and took the elevator to the basement, where the confidential files were kept of all army officers on the active or reserve lists.

Carter took him into his small private office. "I can't let you see the files, Harvey. But I've read them myself. If it's completely off the record—what do you want to know?"

"Any connection either of them has with the Middle East."

"Both. Major Giles Dunton went all through the wartime Middle East campaigns. When the war ended, he was posted to Jerusalem for liaison with the Palestine Police—the time of the troubles. He wasn't used against the Jewish gangs. He went undercover as an Arab."

"How could he?" asked Kennard, startled.

"He had the language. He passed his military proficiency thing in Arabic, during the war, while he was stationed in Cairo. He made several intelligence sorties in Arab dress, in Transjordan, Syria, and all through the Holy Land, and got away undetected. He was one of only about half a dozen British officers to be used in that way."

"Anything like it with the other brother?"

"Not exactly. Captain Mark Dunton is much younger, and wasn't commissioned until 1959."

"Has he served in the Middle East?"

"Yes. He was in Aden during the withdrawal."

"Any language proficiency?"

"Not on his record. He saw a lot of urban guerrilla fighting, and served for a twelvemonth in intelligence.

There's a note that he concentrated on Arab revolutionary organizations."

"In Aden, or all over?"

"It doesn't say. But I expect it'd be all over. They link up."

Kennard rose to go. "Thanks, Jim."

"If you want the files, I have to have high-level authority."

"If it comes to that, you'll get it. I don't want to do anything official yet. So far I'm only playing a hunch. But if I'm right, it could be damn serious."

Back at his own desk, Kennard put through a call to the Dunton house in Dorset.

"Sorry," said the voice at the other end. "Mr. Giles isn't here. It's the farm bailiff speaking. He went up to his London club and is going abroad for a month or two."

"May I have a word with Mrs. Dunton?"

"Sorry again. She isn't here, either. She's gone to London to get a United States visa, to visit her mother in America. Can I take a message?"

"It's not urgent. I'll write."

When he had hung up, he tilted his chair back, frowning. It was all fitting too damn well.

He buzzed for the secretary they all shared. "Did you check on the bank Mark Dunton works in? Good. See if you can raise him."

A few minutes later she came through on his line. "Captain Dunton's out."

"Just out, or away?"

"They said he'd be in later today."

"Thanks," said Kennard. He wrote out a note asking for an interview with Colonel Chase.

§

Anybody who happened to notice Colonel Chase on his morning walk, in all weathers, from his Pimlico flat across St. James's Park into Whitehall would probably take him to be a clerk in a minor government office. He was short, thin, dim-looking, with sparse, straw-colored hair, a small mustache, and pale-gray eyes behind steel-rimmed spectacles. Friends in his clubs knew that his actual background was Winchester and the Guards. But only the most senior men in the Defence Ministry or at Scotland Yard were aware that Colonel Chase was one of the few men outside the cabinet who could report to the Prime Minister direct.

"Well, Kennard?"

"When I went to Dunton's funeral, sir, I met his brothers. I think they want watching."

"Why?"

"I talked to the older one, Giles, the twin, at the house after. I said the obvious thing—let us know if the department could help in any way. He made an odd reply. He said it wasn't a matter for any department."

"So?"

"It worried me, sir. I didn't realize until next day just what was worrying me. It's the implication. Not a matter for a department, but a matter for somebody—for him. You haven't seen him. He's a sullen, scowling man. He looks capable of violence. And there's the thing about twins. . . ."

"You mean, some sort of revenge for his brother's death? But what?"

"I checked on his service record, sir. Quite unofficially. I've a friend—"

Chase smiled. "Don't tell me. How about the record?"

"He's an Arab linguist who served in intelligence in Palestine shortly after the war, and went underground several times as an Arab."

Chase rose and went over to the window, sitting on the sill, hands clasped between his knees, looking toward Kennard.

"I'd better have this straight. You think, on the basis of an odd remark and an old military record, that Dunton is going out to the Middle East to take some kind of revenge on the Palestinians for his brother's death?"

"I think he has already gone, sir."

He told of his phone call.

"What revenge?" asked Chase, musing, as though asking himself. "Presumably a killing. An eye for an eye. So who? A leading Arab? King Hussein, do you think? Or could it even be Nasser?"

"My guess is a Palestinian," said Kennard.

Chase agreed. "More logical. So?"

"It could be George Habbash."

"P.F.L.P. Yes, they're the wild boys. The chap whose bomb killed Dunton was probably one of them."

"But I've checked on Habbash, sir. He's in North Korea, studying revolutionary strategy, he says. So that only leaves one other likely Palestinian."

"Yassir Arafat."

Kennard nodded. "And I reckon he's the most likely. If Giles Dunton is out to even the score for his brother, he's almost certain to go for the best-known name."

Chase rose from the windowsill and began to pace the room, slowly, meditatively. "There's another brother too, isn't there?"

"The youngest. Captain Mark Dunton."

"Is he in it?"

"I don't know, sir. He's still in London. I checked that today. But he could be in it. He served in intelligence in Aden, a specialist in Arab revolutionary groups."

Chase went to his phone. "Get me Marshall. . . . Hello, Chase here. Marshall, I want the personal files of two officers on the reserve list. Major Giles Dunton and his younger brother, Captain Mark Dunton. . . . Yes, it's fairly urgent. Give them the necessary authority, please, and don't bring me into it."

He hung up and resumed his slow pacing. "Look here, Kennard, it's damn thin. You hear a remark which seems to you odd, and draw extravagant conclusions from it. I grant you they look less improbable when you find out about the men themselves."

"It fits too well, sir."

"Not sure that I agree. But if Arafat is even a remote possibility, we dare not risk it. So far as we have any hope in the Palestinian tangle, he's the man. He's competent—which most of them aren't—and by his own lights moderate. If he were killed, the wild boys would certainly take over. There'd be an upsurge of skyjacks, bombings, machine-gun slaughter in airports. Hundreds more innocent people would die, all over Europe and probably the States. God knows where it would end."

"I was going to suggest a quiet check on the obvious air routes, sir, to see if we can pick up Dunton's whereabouts."

"Do that. But keep it discreet. There's one line of inquiry I can make myself. I happen to be a member of the same club as Giles Dunton. I don't use it much, it's not my regular haunt. But I'll look in and see if I can glean anything."

"Permission to make a few more inquiries myself, sir?"

"In what direction?"

"The family."

"All right, Kennard. But go carefully. Nothing obvious."

§

In his newspaper days Kennard had known several publishers. He telephoned Gillet. "Hugh, do you know Helen Dunton?"

"Yes, a little."

"I want to meet her socially when her husband isn't there."

The other laughed. "Very attractive. But, by what I've heard, they're devoted. You're probably wasting your time."

"Okay. But how do I do it?"

"I'll ring you back later today."

The call came within the hour. "You're in luck, Harvey. There's a publishers'-editors' seminar, a sort of teach-in, at the National Book League tomorrow. Helen Dunton's attending the seminar, and it finishes with a party. I'll take you, if you like."

"Remind me that I owe you a favor."

The party was booksy. Kennard groaned softly to himself as Hugh Gillet took him in. As a newspaperman he had been to so many—high-pitched, excited discussions of nothing, and a glass of amontillado sherry.

The drink, however, was better than he had expected. A girl was going around with a tray of gin and whiskey. Relieved, he took a scotch.

"She is over by the window," Gillet told him, "talking to that chap without a beard—distinction enough in this company. I don't know her well. And there are quite a few people here I ought to chat to. So I'll leave it to your celebrated charm."

"Never fails," said Kennard, starting to work through the throng toward Helen Dunton.

She was still talking to the beardless man, so he stood slightly to one side, and waited. Human curiosity never resists that. A few minutes later she glanced toward him, frowning, trying to place him.

"Harvey Kennard," he said. "I was Anthony's colleague, and we were friends. You saw me at the funeral."

"Of course. Now I remember you. Wasn't it an awful family occasion?"

"Grim." He saw that her glass was empty, and that the girl with the tray was near. "Was yours gin or scotch?"

"Gin, please."

He handed her one, took another scotch for himself, and smiled at the girl. The beardless man had turned away to talk to somebody else.

"Did you know Anthony well?" she asked.

"Fairly well. Though he was always a rather shy man, as you know. I met his wife once or twice at parties he gave at his home. How is she taking it?"

"Quite bravely."

"I'd expect that." He took a sip of his drink. "Is your husband here, by the way?"

She laughed. "Not he. He keeps well away from my book world, and I steer clear of his banking chums, who are just about the most unscrupulous, concupiscent body of men in London."

He dutifully grinned, understanding the warning.

"Did you want to see him about anything special?" she asked.

"Nothing urgent. There are one or two matters relating to Anthony I ought to mention to the family. I telephoned Dorset, but it seems that Giles Dunton has gone abroad."

"So I heard. He and Anthony were twins, you know. Giles took it hard."

"It was a ghastly thing. I miss Anthony more than I thought I'd miss anybody. Is your husband away too? I rang his office, but they said he wasn't available."

"He must simply have been out. He does go abroad quite

often for the bank, but he's in London now until he visits Paris, and then Bahrain. Shall I ask him to contact you?"

"Please don't trouble. I'll get at him through the bank. I can probably reach him, either before he goes to Paris, or between the two trips. Do you know his dates?"

"He's going to Paris tomorrow, I think, and staying until Monday or Tuesday. I believe he has a flight booked to Bahrain on the twenty-eighth. It's investment business—oil money."

"Big business."

She agreed. "Are you linked with publishing, Mr. Kennard?"

"Oh, no, I'm here as Hugh Gillet's guest. We're old friends, and he's coming to dinner with me, so he said I'd better get a bit of culture in first," he told her, smiling. "And I see he's beckoning me to meet somebody. Nice to have seen you again, Mrs. Dunton."

§

Next morning there was a note on his desk to see Chase.

"Come in, Kennard. Anything more?"

"Quite a bit, sir. Mark, the younger brother, has booked a flight to Bahrain on the twenty-eighth. Over the previous weekend he's to be in Paris. Both are supposed to be business trips. Paris probably is. The bank has a branch there. But Bahrain . . ."

Chase admitted the point. "I looked in at the club. The day before Giles Dunton left, he was asking for another member, Major Oliphant."

"Oliphant, sir? New name to me. Does it mean much?"

"Yes. He's outside your parish, but not outside mine.

Bruce Oliphant held a commission in the Royal Tank Regiment, from which he retired three years ago and returned to his native province. He's an Ulsterman, of the kind that goes straight back to Carson."

"I'm not with you, sir."

"Oliphant is a fanatical Orangeman. Army intelligence sources in Belfast think he's the man organizing, and probably leading, a violent and vicious Protestant outfit which is just coming to light."

"Why don't they pick him up?"

"They didn't while they had the chance, for political reasons. Now they can't find him. He's gone underground. Since I heard that Giles Dunton was asking for him, I've done a little checking myself. He and Dunton are old friends."

"What's the connection, sir?"

"Just as several terrorist groups in various parts of the world have linked together—particularly the I.R.A., the Palestinians, and the Japanese—so, on the quiet, has the other side. There are intelligence reports of a partnership between extreme right-wing Ulstermen and a shadowy but powerful organization of counterterrorists in Jordan and Lebanon. In Jordan they are thought to be officer class. In Lebanon, business interests."

"So Giles Dunton is trying to find his old friend Oliphant," said Kennard softly, "to arrange for cover, help, and probably weapons in either Lebanon or Jordan. Do you think he has found him?"

"I think he may have. The club porter told Dunton that the only member who could direct him to Oliphant was another retired army officer, a Colonel Hawthorn. Incidentally, nobody suspected Hawthorn of having anything to do with Northern Ireland or the Protestant extremists. Now he's a useful man to watch. Anyway, Dunton found Hawthorn that same day. They talked in the bar of the club."

"Then, sir . . . ?"

"You'd better get across to Belfast."

Kennard made a face. "No passports, no records. It's a bet he's not staying in any hotel."

"Not quite as hopeless as that. You know who our people are over there. A certain amount of surveillance is going on. But it would be as well not to delay."

5

For more than an hour Giles Dunton sat patiently in the shaky armchair by the window of the room in the small public house in Belfast. Nobody came.

What he could see of the view was not enticing; the backs of a terrace of small houses, grimy, unkempt, most of the yards littered with junk, a mongrel dog nosing into the dustbins at the yard gates onto a narrow alley.

Several beer barrels were stacked in the yard of the pub itself. The car in which he had arrived was gone. Near the wooden gate, now secured with an iron bar, a barrel had been adapted as kennel for a large, rough-haired dog, held by a heavy chain; mongrel, but basically Irish wolfhound. It must have been put out there after Giles's arrival.

When another half hour had passed, he rose and went over to the door. It was securely locked. He tried rapping, and calling out a couple of times, "Anyone there?" But there was no response. He returned to the window. The frame was screwed shut from outside. For a moment he was uneasy. He could, of course, break the glass, but then there was quite a drop into the yard. And the dog. Anyway, why should he? He was among friends.

He settled back into the chair. They must be waiting for Bruce to arrive, probably after dark. He looked at his watch; that would mean at least another seven hours. The room was getting uncomfortably hot. He took off his jacket and tie and unbuttoned the collar of his shirt. He was growing thirsty. He went over again to the door, rapping loudly, calling, "Could I have something to drink, please?" No response.

Getting angry, he began to pace the room. Then he noticed, on a shelf beneath a small table, nearly hidden by the cloth, a carafe of water, a glass, and a plate covered by a damp napkin. Beneath the napkin were ham sandwiches. The water was warm, but he drank some gratefully. He was grateful, too, for the sandwiches, although as he ate them he wryly recalled that the last time they met he had stood Bruce Oliphant a damned good dinner, and they had shared a couple of bottles of 1961 Calon Segur. He would remind the bugger of that when he turned up.

It was late afternoon when the door was unlocked and the man who had driven him entered with an apology. "Sorry to have kept you waiting. Major. But we're under orders, you'll understand. If you'll follow me now . . ."

Giles replaced his necktie and jacket with deliberate slowness. Then he nodded to go ahead.

At the foot of the stairs he could see through into the taproom, where a few men were seated with glasses of dark beer on the table. A thin greyhound lay at the feet of one. Sam B. motioned him to continue down the stairs to the cellar, not following him, but closing the oak door at the stairhead.

The steps were of worn stone, dimly lit. A rope handgrip ran down the wall. The narrow passage at the bottom was

47 •

almost dark. Giles took a few uncertain steps—and felt the muzzle of a gun poked into his back. A rough Irish voice behind him murmured, "All right, Major. Stand still now."

Next moment a sack came down over his head, shrouding him to the shoulders.

"What the hell . . . ?" he shouted, muffled in the sack.

But the gun shoved harder into his ribs. "Easy now, Major. Keep straight ahead. The door's open. Keep going until I'm telling you to stop."

Giles moved slowly, stumbling a little, trying desperately to reason. These must be the I.R.A. There must have been a betrayal. But by whom? And, in God's name, why?

Through the opening of the sack at his chest he could see that he was now in a lighted room, stepping across a stone-paved floor. He sensed that there were others in the room, although there was silence.

"Halt," ordered the voice behind him. "Now, Major, raise your arms forward and you'll feel a wall. Put your hands against it, shoulder level, Major, palms flat on the wall."

The wall was of rough brick.

"Now then, Major, feet wide apart. Look sharp."

As he widened his stance, Giles recognized what was happening; the questioning torture there had been so much fuss about in the internment camps.

"Get your feet further back, Major, away from the wall." He felt a sharp kick on his left shin. "Further back. Get the weight on your arms."

The ache was starting already, not so much in the arms as in the shoulders and the small of the back.

Another voice spoke, an educated voice, English rather than Irish. "It's not comfortable, Major Dunton. After about an hour it becomes pretty fair hell. And I warn you not to try anything. There are three of us here, with revolvers to hand on the table. So just stand still. It's up to you how long you stay there. You can stop it simply by giving us truthful answers to a few questions. And they had better be truthful, because we already have enough information to check on them."

"Who are you?" asked Giles suddenly, his voice queerly strained in the muffling of the hood over his head. "I.R.A.?"

His interrogator laughed. "No, we're not the Provos. On the contrary."

"Then what the hell's all this in aid of?" Giles demanded. "If you're the contrary, you're the people I came to see. Where is Major Oliphant?"

He shifted one foot as though to straighten and turn. Immediately there was a punishing kick on his ankle. He yelled—and was livid with himself for yelling. It was the unexpectedness of the pain.

"I warned you," said his interrogator. "The longer you defer the questions, the longer you stand there."

"I demand to see Bruce Oliphant."

"It's not exactly your turn for demanding. What you are going to tell us is who sent you here, for what purpose, and how you knew that Colonel Hawthorn is the link."

Giles was starting to realize how painful this was going to be. The muscles of his shoulders and arms, where the strain was now worst, were already aching acutely. In his right shoulder, where the muscle had once been severed, his old war wound, the pain was like burning. His legs were not as yet much affected, because of their strength. But he well knew that the lumbar ache that was intruding more and more into his consciousness would eventually spread down the muscles and nerves of his thighs. There was the added irritation of the fetid sack over his head which made breathing difficult.

"If you take this bloody hood off, and we sit down together at the table, I'm ready to discuss all that."

"Not a chance. You stay there until you talk."

"Then you can go to hell," replied Giles thickly, and was silent.

"The pain comes gradually at first, I'm told," went on the interrogator's voice pleasantly. "I haven't experienced it myself, but one of us has. Tell him, Fred."

"It's not the telling that'll impress him," put in a third voice, in the whining accent of Ulster, "but the feeling of it. Just wait awhile. And keep quiet. Talking helps distract it."

"I'll time it then," came the interrogator's voice. "Silence for five minutes before the first question."

The silence seemed interminable. Giles feared that his right shoulder might give and he would fall. Anger was accumulating within him, and he used it to stiffen his resistance to the steady crescendo of pain that reached now from his forearms down his back to his thighs. He forced himself to think of Anthony. The pain he was suffering was nothing compared to the torture Anthony's frail body must have endured when he was betrayed to the Gestapo. That reinforced him. He muttered to himself, in the stifling darkness of the sack, that they could do what they bloody well liked. He would not give in.

"Five minutes," announced the voice of the interrogator. "Now the first question. Who told you that Colonel Hawthorn could put you in touch with Major Oliphant?"

Giles was silent. The question was repeated three times. He remained silent.

"Very well then, we must wait for that answer. Second question. Whom are you working for? The army? Or is it the department your brother belonged to? In the end you're going to tell us, Major Dunton."

Giles made no sound.

"Very well. Ten minutes for reflection."

It would seem like an hour, Giles knew. His whole body was now a pulsing of pain. Only with difficulty could he keep his head from sagging. But he no longer needed distraction. He had built up a sullen rage by which he would endure it for as long as these sods kept him there—endure it without speaking a word. So long as he remained conscious, he would stand there in silence.

"Ten minutes. I'll put the first question again. Who told you that Colonel Hawthorn could direct you to Major Oliphant?" After a pause. "Why be stubborn? You can't keep silent in the end. Nobody can."

"Repeat the questions now," said the Ulster voice. "Keep on with them regular, like a clock."

So the questions were repeated, time after time, inexorably. Giles began to lose the meaning of them, even the words. They beat upon his hearing like blows upon his tormented muscles, rhythmical, unavoidable, searing. How long it was going on he scarcely knew any more, his sense of time misting. He feared that his consciousness might be slipping, and he held it within him by a tautening of will. But it was slipping.

What roused him was a sudden clatter, a question broken off, the door opening, and a new voice, "There's a patrol coming down the street, infantry and a couple of armored cars."

"Are they searching the houses?"

"Not all, but some. Better get away."

"What are we to do with him?"

"Shoot the bastard," came the Ulster growl.

"No," from the interrogator, sharply. "Turn him round."

Giles felt his arms knocked upward, so that he fell

forward, striking his head on the wall, sliding down to the floor. He was seized under the arms and jerked upright.

"You're going back to the bedroom," said the interrogator. "The door will not be locked. If the troops search this building, and find you, I warn you not to make contact with them. Say you're a commercial staying in the house. Say anything you like. But if you either try to get away, or declare yourself to the patrol, there will be retribution. Not here, Major Dunton, but back at your home in England, or wherever your family may be."

He had to be half carried up the cellar stairs, stumbling, then up the house stairway. At the top he was shoved hard in the back. He went sprawling across the floor. The door was closed behind him. By the time he had raised his head and pulled away the sack, he was alone in the room from which he had been taken.

He got himself to the window, supporting himself on the chair. The huge dog was now loose, roaming threateningly around the yard. He could make out a couple of infantrymen moving, widely spaced, weapons at the ready, along the cover of the housefronts on the far side of the street, and could hear the engine of the car.

Declare himself! He muttered angrily. Why did not the stupid bastards understand that the one thing he certainly could not do was to identify himself to anybody, let alone to the army?

§

The department car that brought Harvey Kennard to Herne Hill was waiting while he went up to his flat to pack a hasty suitcase, and would then take him to Heathrow.

Sally was in the kitchen, making herself some lunch. "Do you want any?"

"Sorry, love. No time. I'm off on a job."

She came through to the bedroom. "How long will you be away?"

"You know that's a silly question."

Suddenly her exasperation overcame caution. "What have you done to Maurice?"

"Maurice? What could I possibly have done?"

"He hasn't been here for a fortnight, or even phoned. Every time I ring his office I get a brush-off. It's like you to resent my friends. You always have."

He understood why she had now come out with it. His absence would clear the way for her current boyfriend; and he was not showing up.

Kennard knew, of course, of her occasional strayings. He tolerated them because, he reasoned, he must be in love with her. She was faithful for the first couple of years of their marriage, but then boredom set in. The strayings became more frequent when she reached her thirties, and now her forties were not far off. Kennard understood how the vain, silly creature he loved craved for youthfulness. So he ignored her wanderings. But the latest, with Maurice, was more than he could take—a smooth-faced illiterate who made money by buying up old London rooming houses, ejecting the tenants by methods which were better not discussed, and converting them into flashy-looking flats for sale. And arrogant and condescending with it. Maurice got him raw.

"I even rang his home," said Sally defiantly. "His wife answered. She sounded as big a bitch as he says she is."

"Did you try phoning his girl friend?"

He saw by her look that she had not known.

"Maurice is keeping a girl in one of his flats in Streatham," he told her.

"I don't believe you."

Kennard shrugged. "I made a few inquiries. It wasn't difficult. And I'll tell you, since you insist, what I did to Maurice. I told him that, unless he stopped hanging round you, I'd introduce his wife to his mistress. That's why you haven't seen Maurice lately, and won't see him any more."

She was on the edge of tears. He put his arm around her shoulders, but she shook away.

"I'm sorry to spring it on you when we can't discuss it," he said. "But you brought it up. You asked the question. Now I've simply got to go. I'll call you directly I know when I'll be back. Take care of yourself."

He was moody in the car on the way to the airport, not saying much to the driver. He was wondering sadly how long he and Sally would be able to stay together, or whether the break had already arrived, needing only to be admitted.

A car was waiting for him at Aldergrove. It took him to a small office at the rear of a block near the city center. He noted with grim curiosity the battered houses, the gaps where bombs had demolished buildings, the blackened interior of shops gutted by incendiaries; and with admiration the apparently stolid attitude of people walking the streets.

He had not previously met Ferris, the man he had come to see; a large, stout man with a rubicund face and thick gray hair. But he knew of him, of course, and Ferris had been told of his errand. "It seems pretty hopeless. We have a few people wandering about the airport and the steamer terminals, well briefed on wanted men. We've picked up several."

"Unfortunately, my man isn't one of the wanted."

"There's still a chance. If our chaps see anyone behaving

oddly, or in contact with somebody they know about, they get photographs. We have these tiny Jap cameras with incredible range." Ferris opened a file on his desk. "The portraits aren't brilliant, but usually they're identifiable."

"Anybody in the past few days?"

"Not many." Ferris passed over the file. "Two at the airport and three from the ferry."

Kennard picked up the print of the man seated on the bench in the front hall at Aldergrove. It was faint, fuzzy, out of focus, but unmistakable. "That's Dunton."

Ferris consulted a sheet of typed notes. "Then you're in luck. We know the man who met him. He's a taxi driver named Sam Boylan, and he's linked with the extremists of the right. Our chap at Aldergrove had noticed your man waiting there, and had been watching him for some time. When he saw Boylan approaching him, he managed to get that picture."

"Can we find the taxi driver?"

"Sure." Ferris dialed a number. "I know the garage he works from. Hello. Hello. Ah, is Mr. Boylan around? You're expecting him soon? No, no message. Nothing important." He hung up. "My car's down below."

The garage stood in a side street. Ferris parked opposite. A few minutes later he nodded to Kennard as an old Morris came around the corner and entered the garage.

"No point in approaching him," said Ferris. "It'd alert them, and he'd simply say a customer phoned a rank for a taxi, and he picked him up at Aldergrove and drove him to the station, or someplace like that. If we tail him, he may lead us to your man."

"Worth trying," Kennard agreed. "I don't want to pick Dunton up, you understand—just to know where he is, and where he goes. There's nothing to face him with anyway. So long as he stays in Ireland, we're not worried. It's when he moves on . . ."

The Morris was coming out of the garage. Ferris let it turn the corner, then started after it. Not far away it stopped at a block of flats, picked up an elderly woman with a large suitcase, and drove on.

After a few minutes, Ferris said, "I think this is a genuine customer. He's making for the station." He picked up a police-wave microphone and warned that if an elderly woman in blue costume and blue felt hat arrived shortly by taxi at the station, she'd better be stopped and the suitcase examined before she got on a train—but not until the taxi had moved away.

"Probably some old biddy off for a few days with her married daughter. But in this town, with suitcases, you never know."

The taxi pulled up at the station entrance. The old woman got out, paid the driver, and found a porter to take her case. The taxi drove off, Ferris following.

After a few more minutes he said, "I think we may be on track. He's heading into one of the strongest Protestant districts. I'm ready to bet his next stop isn't for a customer."

Nor was it. Turning through several back streets, the Morris pulled up outside a small public house and Boylan went in.

"Just to get himself a beer?" asked Kennard.

"Could be. But we know his associations, and we know the character of this district. If you add them together . . ."

He was reaching for the car microphone, but Kennard checked him. "What are you going to do?"

"Lay on a surveillance of the pub."

Kennard demurred. "It's a small pub, serving the surrounding streets. Strangers would rouse suspicion at once."

"What then?"

"Keep clear of the pub and put a tail on Boylan and his taxi. If the pub is the meeting place, and Dunton is hidden there, they'll almost certainly bring in Boylan when he moves. That's all I want to know—when he moves, and where he goes."

§

It was Giles Dunton's fourth day in the pub bedroom. Twice each day a man came in with a meal. The man's face was hidden in a balaclava-style knitted brown mask, and in his free hand he carried a revolver. Each time he put down the tray in silence, and made no reply to the questions which Giles shouted at him. "What the hell's going on? Where's Major Oliphant?"

He contemplated escape. But why should he? This was the contact he had come to make. Bruce Oliphant must turn up. It must be his arrival they were awaiting.

When it grew dark there was nothing to stay awake for. He was already dozing when the door opened and the light snapped on. The hooded man who brought his food stood in the doorway, the gun in his hand. "Come on down. You're wanted."

For a moment Giles contemplated rushing him. But the chances were too slight. He shrugged, put on his jacket, and went downstairs, the man behind him with the revolver. On ground level he wondered if he could bolt through the taproom into the street, but he knew he would never make it. So he went down the cellar stairs.

The passage below was lit and the cellar door open. Three other hooded men sat at the table inside. The man who had brought him down closed the door, stood against it, and kept his revolver ready.

The center man at the table began, in the educated English voice Giles had heard on the last occasion. "We know now that you're working for the department in which your brother served."

"If that's your information, it's false. I'm not."

"Our information is reliable enough, Dunton. We have contacts in the security organizations in Belfast—not difficult for Protestants. I suppose you're going to deny knowing a man named Harvey Kennard."

"Kennard? Kennard? Oh, yes, I do know him. He was one of my brother's colleagues and he came to the funeral. That's the only time I've met him."

"Sufficient time to recruit you."

"Oh, come on," Giles protested. "This is all bloody nonsense. I've not been recruited into anything. I've come here to see Bruce Oliphant on a personal matter."

"If Colonel Hawthorn hasn't been blown, and you're not working for Whitehall, how did you know he could put you in touch with Major Oliphant?"

"It happens that we all three belong to the same club. I inquired there."

"You expect us to believe that?"

Giles said nothing.

After a pause, the interrogator asked, "Would it surprise you to know that Harvey Kennard arrived in Belfast this morning?"

"Not particularly. It has nothing to do with me."

"Since Kennard arrived, a security tail has been put on the man who brought you here. He'll keep clear of the place now, naturally."

Giles remained cool. "You're making unwarranted

assumptions. Kennard may well have come on security business connected with you people, and with your courier. He hasn't come on my account. I covered my trail. Nobody, other than yourselves, could possibly know I'm here."

"Nobody except the department that sent you."

"I tell you, that's complete nonsense."

"Shoot the bugger now," cut in a second man at the table in an Ulster accent. "We can dump him in a Catholic area. My car's round the corner."

"It's what I'm inclined to do," mused the interrogator. Turning to the third man, he asked, "Well?"

The third man pulled the hood from his head and said, "What do you want of me, Giles? And how did you know that Hawthorn could tell you where I am?"

Giles stared at him. "Were you here when I was stood against that wall?"

"No," said Oliphant. "I was leading a sortie into the Republic. There's a rest house for some of the Provisionals near Buncrana, a little place on Lough Swilly. We had to hole up for four nights before we could slip in among them. We got three and a possible fourth. I came back here only an hour ago. If I'd been here when you were brought in, I'd have stopped the interrogation. But you can't blame them, Giles. If Hawthorn really is blown to British security, it's damn serious for us. How did you get on to him?"

"Arthur."

Oliphant laughed loudly. "Fair enough." To the others he explained, "Arthur's the club porter. His knowledge of the affairs of all the members is legendary. He would certainly have known, or guessed from observation, that Hawthorn and I are in cahoots. It's all right, I tell you. Hawthorn isn't blown, and Dunton isn't working for Whitehall. Sit down, Giles, and tell me what you've come

59 •

for." He gestured to the man by the door. "Bring over a chair for Major Dunton, and put that gun away." To the other men at the table he added, "It's safe enough to take off your hoods, unless you're too shy."

As Giles sat down opposite, they hesitated, then pulled off the hoods. The interrogator was fair-haired, probably in his mid-twenties, with a long, sensitive face, high forehead, steady blue eyes. The other was a ginger-haired, rough, surly man of middle age with badly fitting dentures and a scar over one cheek.

"If you've nothing to do with British intelligence," this last man asked, "why is Kennard in Belfast, and why is Sam Boylan being tailed?"

"So help me," Giles assured him, "I simply don't know. It can't be anything to do with me."

"Why are you here?" asked Oliphant.

Giles looked doubtfully at the others, but Oliphant gestured him to go on.

"You read about Anthony, of course."

Oliphant murmured regrets.

"Mark and I intend to even the score."

"How?"

"By getting the Palestinian commander, and letting it be known that it's a revenge killing. Yassir Arafat. He now practically runs Jordan. The little king's almost helpless, with refugees forming half his population, twelve thousand Iraqi troops stationed in his country, and the Syrians massing tanks on his frontier. But you know all that."

Oliphant nodded. "You think you could do it?"

"I think it can only be done by individuals. No government will act. It brings on more hijacked aircraft, more threats to hostages, more slaughter. So these wild bastards, probably pepped up on hashish, can go on killing people with little fear of punishment. But not forever. Anthony's death isn't going unpunished. And when a few more murders like that have been revenged on the men leading the terrorists, enthusiasm will dry up fast. Damn it, Bruce, it's what you're starting to do here, isn't it?"

"So that's why you came," mused Oliphant. "Our talk over dinner a few weeks ago."

"Of course. You didn't actually say in so many words that you are linking with people of similar views elsewhere, but it's what I took you to be hinting."

"What do you want of us?"

"To be put into touch with your friends in the Middle East, and to be able to get hold of weapons there. Smuggling them by air is too risky, and trying to get them past half a dozen land frontiers isn't practical. And I want a safe house in or near Beirut and another in Jordan, preferably in Amman."

"I'll give you one name," said Oliphant. "Louis Mouzouri. He's a Lebanese banker." He took a notebook from his pocket, wrote in it, tore out the page, and handed it to Giles. "That's his house, a few miles south of Beirut, lovely place. He's very rich. When do you expect to get there?"

"At the beginning of next month."

"That gives me time to warn Mouzouri. He has contacts in Jordan, mostly army officers. Are you flying out?"

"Mark is. I'm going by sea from Marseilles."

"And how are you proposing to get away from here?"

Giles looked surprised. "Why should there be a problem?"

Oliphant leaned back in his chair. "You're underestimating them, Giles. I've more experience than you. Kennard hasn't come to Belfast after us. There's a security outfit stationed here that looks after us. It's you."

"It can't be," protested Giles uneasily. "He can't know anything because, so far, there's nothing to know."

Oliphant shook his head. "He must or he wouldn't be here. They'll be looking for you at all the points of departure. Once they've spotted you, you won't shake them off. Your only chance is to duck Kennard now."

"How?"

"We'll see you over the border into the Republic. It had better be tonight. Fred, your car, and take the Z route."

The Ulsterman grunted. He looked sour. But he did not refuse.

"How does it help?" objected Giles.

"They won't yet be watching the exit points from the Republic. You can get back into England, or better still go straight to France without being picked up. I take it you've got your passport with you. Nobody at Dublin airport pays any special attention to British passports, they're common enough. Plenty of U.K. citizens live in Eire." He turned to the sentinel by the door. "Get Major Dunton something to eat, and a bottle of whisky to take with him. Better have the meal in your bedroom, Giles. Be ready in an hour."

§

It was dusk when the Ulsterman drove him away. The sky was overcast, the street lamps thin. Away to the east a red glow flickered in the sky. Giles nudged the driver, who said briefly, "The Provos set off a car bomb two hours ago outside a furniture store."

Little more was said for more than an hour. Then the car turned off the road onto a muddy farm track, and the driver dowsed the lights. "Here's where we cross. The main roads are guarded and the side roads obstructed. Stay here while I find out if there's any danger of a patrol."

He slid out of the car and into the darkness. Half an hour passed before he as silently returned.

"They told me at the farm that a patrol was just due. I had to lie up until it passed. All's clear now."

Traveling with only sidelights, the car bumped along a rough track, then lurched across pasture. A gap in the far hedge opened onto a narrow lane.

"Here's where they patrol. The border's just ahead."

The Ulsterman stopped the car to open a gate on the other side of the lane, closing it after the car was through onto a track through a wood. Ten minutes later he switched on his headlights and turned into another lane, then not long after onto a country road.

"Are we across?" asked Giles.

"Aye. This is the Republic."

They drove in silence for another hour, Giles looking out sleepily at the dark countryside. The sky was clearing to starlight. The car's lamps wandered over flat fields, empty bogs, occasional whitewashed cottages. He was aware of the looming shadow of distant mountains.

They turned between stone gateposts onto a long drive to a small Georgian farmhouse, backed by barns. The Ulsterman drove the car inside one of them, and led Giles across a cluttered farmyard to a back door. An elderly man opened to them and took them to a room under the roof, with two beds. Giles pulled out the whisky bottle and they shared the one tooth glass. Then each took a bed, the Ulsterman removing his dentures and placing them under his pillow. Giles drank some more of the peaty whisky, trying to sleep in spite of the Ulsterman's snoring.

They lay up all day and set off again at dark along the

lonely Irish roads. Before dawn they were hidden in a house just north of Dublin. On Monday morning, soon after ten o'clock when the traffic was moving freely, the Ulsterman drove him to another house in a southern suburb; the busiest daylight hours were the safest in which to cross the city.

There was only a girl in the house; her father was out. She got them a meal and left them alone.

"I want a tourist-class ticket on the next flight from Dublin to Paris," Giles told the Ulsterman. "I've got cash, but it's in English notes. Will they take them at a travel office?"

"Best let me get the ticket for you. I'll change the notes at a bank. They could be looking for you even down here. What name will I buy the ticket in? Not your own."

"But my passport—"

"The man who looks at your passport doesn't look at the passenger list. They're not that thorough."

Giles smiled. "Fine. Any name you like. Richard Trevor, say."

When he came back with the tickets, the Ulsterman told him the first flight he could get him on was the next day at 15:20 hours. "It's the holiday season. You'd best stay holed up here until tomorrow. I'll drive you to the airport."

"Thanks," said Giles. "You've been a great help."

For the first time the Ulsterman smiled. "It'd have been easier to shoot you before Major Oliphant got back."

6

Harvey Kennard hung around Ferris's office, waiting for reports on the taxi driver's movements. They arrived every hour, and varied little. He was picking up occasional customers and driving them to the station, or the airport, or the shopping center. He made several journeys by himself into Protestant districts, stopping each time at a different pub for a drink. Kennard began to wonder whether they were watching the wrong man.

Then early on Monday morning one of Ferris's men hired Boylan's taxi to take him to the airport. The tail car was following. As they got farther from the city and traffic thinned, the man in the taxi saw Boylan glance several times at the image in his driving mirror, and smile to himself derisively.

So he knew. Which meant that Dunton, and the men he was visiting, also knew.

Kennard got through on the scrambler line to Colonel Chase in London. "I think we've missed him, sir. Worse than that, he knows we're onto him."

"How?"

"Not sure, sir. It could be a leak over here. Quite a few have necessarily been involved, and Ferris admits that Belfast's a damn difficult place to keep a secret. If he came here for what we suppose, there's nothing to keep him here this long. We've a watch on all exit points, and they have his picture. He hasn't shown up."

"You think he has gone into hiding?"

"No. I think he has slipped over the border into the Republic, and gone on from there. We'll probably have to pick him up in England. But just on the off chance I'd like to go down to Dublin myself tomorrow."

"All right. I'll send word to the appropriate quarter in the Defence Ministry in Dublin. The man you'll have to contact is R. K. Sullivan. Keep up the watch on all Ulster exit points and tell Ferris to report to me at once if Dunton is seen."

Kennard caught an early train to Dublin next morning. At the Defence Ministry the ground was prepared. Seated with Sullivan was a plainclothesman from the Garda. "Micháel Ó Braonáin—Mike Brennan to you," said Sullivan, grinning. "He'll take you wherever you want to go and provide any authority you may need. But what in the name of the saints do you hope to find? It's impossible, Mr. Kennard. If the man came here, which he may well have done, he could have used any of the routes to England with no identification whatsoever."

"Extreme Protestant contacts?"

"Here in Dublin? Yes, there are a few. But we'd be reluctant to put you onto them, because it'd give away what we know."

Kennard sighed. "Point taken, sir. I've a few copies of a snap of Dunton. I'll simply have to see what I can do around the exit points with them."

Sullivan grinned. "And the best of British luck!"

They started with the steamer terminal. But all the approaches were jammed with holiday travelers. Brennan handed out a few of the photographs to the port police. It was evident from their quizzical looks that scant attention would be paid to them.

"The airport then," said Brennan. "That's a little more hopeful. Airlines keep passenger lists."

On the drive out he suggested stopping for a sandwich and a couple of pots. "In August, the airport terminal's stuffed with people."

As indeed it was—crowds of perspiring people, stacked luggage, excited children, tired parents waiting for news through the loudspeakers of flights which were mostly delayed. Brennan led the way to the various airline offices, asking whether the name of Dunton appeared on any of the passenger lists during the past two or three days. Mostly he met incredulous looks. Could he really want a search made on an August afternoon? He produced his identity card and insisted. So in each office girls were set to search.

"We'll be back later. Grateful for your help."

Brennan led Kennard toward the departure lounge. "There's a separate desk for British passports. They don't take names, but they do look at faces. It's just worth showing the man the photograph."

"It won't have been the same man on duty all the time."

Brennan sighed. "It's an imperfect world for policemen."

The official at the desk was a big, handsome, curly-haired Irishman. He looked doubtfully at the photograph. "It's a poor print."

"It is that," Brennan agreed. "But it's all we have, seemingly."

The official pondered. "I've a feeling of having seen him through here."

"Recently?"

"It's hard to remember. So many go through. It could be yesterday. Or yet again it could be today."

"You've no idea what flight?"

The official spread his hands deprecatingly. "How could I, and so many people on the move? Would you like to go through to the departure lounge and look around for yourself?"

"Might as well," agreed Brennan.

So as Giles Dunton came out of the men's washroom he caught a glimpse of Kennard and some other man, walking slowly in his direction, peering into the crowds.

Giles turned back to the washroom, careful not to move hastily. He bolted himself into a cabinet and waited.

Ten minutes later his flight was called; boarding through Gate Two. He could give it a little longer. At the third boarding call he knew he would have to risk it. He came out of the washroom, wary. At first he could not see Kennard. Then he spotted him, with the other man, turning their backs as they walked toward the entrance barrier.

Giles moved deliberately along the hall, taking an oblique route toward Gate Two. As he passed onto the apron, and the air hostess noted his ticket and made a tick on her list against Mr. Richard Trevor, so that he could join the line of passengers ascending the gangway stairs into the aircraft, Kennard and Brennan were edging back through the entrance barrier, preparing for a tour of the airline offices in quest of the name Dunton on a passenger list. Hopeless!

§

It worked as easily at Orly airport, Giles found to his relief, as it had at Dublin. When the air hostess handed him an entry form, he filled in the correct number of his passport, a fictitious address, and signed it Richard Trevor. Thousands of such forms are filled every day in airliners all over the world; he was banking on a remark he had once heard from an official, that nobody ever reads them.

At the passport desk at Orly the official glanced casually at him, checking his appearance with the passport photograph. He was through, unrecorded.

He handed in his passport at the hotel and reverted to his actual identity. The hotel registration form, which would go to the local police, would be the only evidence he had entered France. There would be a record, too, at Marseilles when he left. But even if Anthony's department were looking for him, he doubted they would ever get around to finding those two records. The risk was not worth worrying about.

He went up to his room to freshen, and to exchange the British and Irish notes in his pocketbook for some of the francs he had stowed in the inner compartment of his holdall. Then he went out.

It was hot, even in the evening. The streets were as lively as ever. He sat outside a café and drank a Pernod very slowly, watching the Parisian kaleidoscope. The small restaurant he knew best was only a couple of blocks away. It was nearly empty; only five other diners, two couples and a stout man solitary. Giles took a table in the embrasure of the window and lazily asked the waiter, who vaguely remembered him from times past, what he should eat. Something simple. So he started with artichoke hearts in a vinaigrette sauce, with a slice of foie gras; then quenelles de brochet, with which he drank half a bottle of Meursault.

On his way back to the hotel he sat under the trees outside a boulevard café to drink a cognac. A woman invited him, but he shook his head.

Next morning he began his drive south, taking the

journey leisurely, avoiding main motor roads and hotels. That night he drove his car into a wood on a lonely mountain slope near Veynes and laid out on the dry ground the sleeping bag he had stowed in the car. By noon next day he reached a garage on the outskirts of Marseilles, where he had arranged to leave the car. He paid the garage charge for two months.

He took a taxi to the center of the city and found a large brasserie where he could eat, wash, and shave. Then he took another taxi to the docks.

The *Montélimar* was not much of a ship to look at; paintwork indifferent, a few crewmen in stained sweatshirts leaning on the forward rails, and, when Giles ascended the gangway carrying his grip and entered the corridor to the office of the *agent comptable,* a curious mixed smell of garlic and sea water. But the cabin into which he was shown looked comfortable enough, and the bedding was clean. He completed the formalities of embarkation, then went up on deck to watch her making ready to cast off.

Most of the passengers gathering on the rails seemed to be French families, several with young children. There were a few indeterminate men traveling alone, probably minor officials or businessmen returning to their work in Lebanon or Egypt after vacations in France.

The ship's siren sounded a warning of departure. A few men on the dockside were busy with the gangway and the ropes. The engines were turning now, and the first indications of a wash foamed gently in the dirty water. The siren reiterated, the ship edged slowly out.

Giles smiled. He was away.

A girl leaning on the rail near him turned her head and asked, "Isn't it a thrill, watching a ship move off?"

"Never fails," he agreed, looking more closely at her. The voice was American, probably New York. She was darkish-blond, cheerful-featured, dressed in gypsy-style skirt, bodice, and shawl, a decorated leather bandeau around her head. But not exactly hippie, he thought; not unkempt enough.

"You're English?" she asked. "I thought so. We're probably the only two on board speaking English."

"Maybe."

"When I'm abroad I like traveling the way local people travel," she told him. "Out of the tourist groove. I'm on vacation. Are you?"

He nodded. She had, he noticed, a rounded figure beneath that shawl.

"On vacation from college," she volunteered. "My name's Shirley. Mostly I'm called Shirle."

He allowed himself a slow smile. She seemed eager enough and, after all, there were five days of voyaging with nothing much to do.

"Mine's Giles," he told her. "Have you fixed yourself up yet with a place in the dining saloon? No? Come along then, let's go down and do that."

§

The sea was calm; a summer storm sweeping across the Gulf of Lyons petered out behind them. The *Montélimar* was slow but steady, the food as "super" as the travel agent with the charming teeth had promised, and the passengers behaved with the quiet decorum of the bourgeois French; none of the dancing and organized jollity of an Anglo-Saxon cruise ship, not even shuffleboard (although some of the men, in their flat white caps, spent the mornings tossing heavy rubber rings onto numbered squares painted on the deck).

During the day the sun never veiled and there were scant

breezes. At night the sky glowed with stars; the new moon was still a few nights off. On the first evening, after the meal, Giles took the American girl up to the boat deck to show her the limpid brilliance of the sky. Leaning on the rail, he began leisurely to fondle, then to kiss her.

He did it, he told himself good-humoredly, to shut her up, rather than for any sexual urgency. God, she was a talkative girl! Throughout the meal she had kept up a monologue, giving him her opinions with verve. She was a fervent advocate of women's lib. At one time, she told him, she had burned her bra, but for her it had not been comfortable. "My breasts are so heavy that, if I moved faster than a walk, they swung too much. Also I developed a sweat rash underneath. So I had to go back to a bra. But after all, as I said to Eleanor—she's a close friend of mine at college—it's the principle that counts, not the symbol."

One or two of the men, Giles noticed, were glancing at her with curiosity. Their wives were paying her no attention; probably the wives could not understand English.

That was as well, he thought, amused, for she was descanting on freedom. She was very strong for every kind of freedom. There should certainly, she insisted, be freedom to use drugs; not that she herself needed them. Sexual freedom she took to be self-evident. Her own experiences had not begun until she reached college, and then under the tutelage of Eleanor, who was a sophisticate. She confessed that she still felt occasional qualms, and had not entirely conquered the complex of guilt bred into her by her parents (a wholesale grocery merchant and his conventional wife). Shirle herself would one day, no doubt, decide to marry and settle for a family. But meanwhile she regarded sexual experiment as part of her college education, integral to the formation of her mind and personality. Didn't Giles agree?

He assented, smiling. It was all said with such an air of

innocence. Beneath the shawl, the gypsy bodice, and the advanced opinions she uttered, was a cheerful, ordinary girl with a healthy body and uncomplicated mind. In a few years, he guessed, she would be presiding at women's luncheon clubs, like her mother. But meanwhile there was this undaunted acceptance of life—courage, you could call it. See how she was wandering off, on her own, full of innocent trust in humanity and goodness, into the most turbulent, vicious, hate-filled corner of the world.

Lazily he let her prattle on. And how she prattled! Even up here on the boat deck she was discoursing on the stars, naming the constellations, pointing to various individual brilliancies. Giles, who had practiced desert navigation by night, realized she had fair astronomical knowledge. But he was getting bored. So he began to fondle her, without much response.

"About that sexual freedom . . ." he said.

After a pause she answered, as though indifferent, "There's no reason why not."

"Wouldn't it be more comfortable in a cabin?"

"A French girl is sharing mine."

"Nobody in mine," he said. "It's only one deck down."

She was not a particularly good lay. She stripped out nonchalantly enough and climbed into the bunk in his cabin, but then remained passive, almost uninterested; and still loquacious. "This is the first time," she told him, "that I've been to bed with an Englishman."

When he released her, and rolled over onto his back beside her, she started on anecdotal reminiscence, mostly of the exploits of Eleanor. Giles did not bother to listen. One part of Shirle's college education, he murmured to himself, would benefit from extra tuition. There were still four more nights before the *Montélimar* put in at Beirut.

By noon on Wednesday Kennard was convinced that he would find no trace of Giles Dunton in Dublin. But Mike Brennan urged him to stay for a party at his house that evening. He phoned Ferris in Belfast; nothing to report. He phoned London. Nothing had been seen of Major Dunton either at the Dorset house or at the London club. If he had crossed into the Republic and traveled out from there, why had he not shown up in England? The answer was uncomfortably clear, Kennard gloomily told himself. He had gone into hiding, preparatory to his move to the Middle East.

Mike Brennan called his party a hooley—originally, he explained, the name of a Hindu festival in honor of Krishna, having something to do with milkmaids; the Irish version had absolutely nothing to do with milk, and only dubiously with maids. On Thursday morning Kennard woke with the worst hangover he could recall. He went groaning to the airport, stuffed with aspirin and awash with coffee, to fly back to London.

Even altitude didn't help much.

The first check to make, when he reached the department, was on Mark, the younger brother. He called the bank. After some delay the girl told him Captain Dunton was not available, he was away.

Kennard put down the phone, thoughtful. He looked up the number of Helen Dunton's publishing house and dialed that. Mrs. Dunton was not in the office that day.

"I'm a friend of her brother-in-law and I have a message for her, rather important. Can you tell me where I can find her?"

"She's at home, reading manuscripts."

He found Mark Dunton's address and phone number in the directory. When he dialed it, a woman's voice answered, Cockney. Mrs. Dunton was out shopping. This was the domestic help. She thought Mrs. Dunton would be home about tea time.

Kennard passed the time clearing any accumulation of routine office work, and subduing his hangover with beer. At half past three he took the district train from Westminster to Fulham Broadway and walked round the corner into Walham Grove, that avenue of Victorian villas that had, of late years, been thoroughly gentrified; a young advertising executive or a promising film director behind the net curtains of every second window, and alternate front doors vulgarized with brass carriage lamps.

The Duntons' was one of the smaller houses, charmingly if somewhat eccentrically painted, and garnished with pots of scarlet geraniums and deep-blue lobelia. Helen, in slacks and blue linen shirt, opened the door, recognized him, and, after a moment of doubt, asked him in. The living room, all stripped pine, vivid modern art, crowded bookshelves, and an expensive hi-fi deck, ran from front to back of the ground floor; a hint of a small garden through the rear window. The floor was littered with typescripts, pads of paper jotted with notes, large ashtrays.

Helen motioned him to a low seat, switched off the murmur of the hi-fi, and asked what he wanted.

"I've missed your husband again, Mrs. Dunton. I had to go away for a few days—to Northern Ireland," he added deliberately, but there was no tremor of reaction. "I got back to London only this morning and rang his office, but they told me he's away. Is he still in Paris?"

"No. He came back on Tuesday. Yesterday he went on his business trip to Bahrain."

"I thought you said that was to be on the twenty-eighth."

"Did I?" she asked vaguely. "I must have got the date wrong. It was yesterday he left. It was rather a rush, since he got back from France only the day before. I went to Heathrow to pick him up, to save a little time. He left Giles's car in Paris."

"His brother's car?"

"He took it over for him. Giles was in France, and he suddenly decided to go off motoring, but his car was in London, so he rang Mark and asked him to bring it over. He knew Mark was going to Paris on business."

And that, of course, was it, Kennard realized. Giles must have been uncertain of getting in Jordan the weapons he wanted, so he had picked them up in Belfast. How he got them out of Ireland into France was a puzzle, but that's what he must have done. Why else should he want to drive to the Middle East? Whatever the weapons were—probably precision rifles—he must have them stowed somewhere in the body of the car, sufficiently well to get through several frontier posts. Kennard contemplated with dismay the chase that now confronted him.

He became aware that Helen Dunton was looking at him curiously; that he had been caught off guard.

"Is anything wrong, Mr. Kennard?"

"Oh no, nothing wrong."

But he knew, even as he made it, that the answer wouldn't do.

"What did you want to see my husband about?"

"Nothing particularly important."

"Oh, come," she said, "I'm not an idiot. Of course it's important. You have sought me out twice. And just now you looked—"

In desperation he told her, "It's not about your husband, but his brother."

"Anthony? No? You mean Giles? What about him?"

"Sorry, but I can't discuss that."

"Is it to do with Anthony's death?"

"Sorry."

"It must be. Something that Anthony left behind, some information that affects the family? Something that Giles has to do . . . ?" He saw her eyes widen, as though with fright. "Something he's going to do?"

Kennard was silent.

"Is there anything I can do?" she asked, whispering.

"If you get any inkling of where Major Dunton is, tell me. It's simply that we want to discuss something with him, something that could be important. Here are two phone numbers that will always reach me. If I'm not there myself, you can talk quite freely to the person who answers the phone."

He got up to go. He wanted to get out before she asked him any more questions. He was wondering how much he had already compromised, uneasily recalling Colonel Chase's instruction to be particularly cautious with the family.

§

"I heard of it only this afternoon when I saw her," Kennard told Colonel Chase. "It must mean he already has the guns or whatever, and he's got them stowed in his car."

"There must be a dozen frontiers. It's mad."

"It depends on which way he goes, sir. All his choices except one involve an Iron Curtain country, or Yugoslavia."

"Which one doesn't?"

"France into Italy, then the car ferry from Brindisi to Greece. But then he's got Turkey, and the Turks are tough and thorough. I can't see him risking it."

"Couldn't he get his car shipped direct from Greece to the Lebanon?"

"I think it can be done, sir, but not without a lot of organization. If he tries that, I don't see how we can miss him. There's the alternative of North Africa. He could get his car across from either France or Spain. But then he has the whole gamut of Arab countries to cross."

"If his target's Arab," Chase pointed out, "that might be the obvious route. Suppose he's going for Nasser."

Kennard shook his head. "If the basic idea's right, I think it must be Arafat, which means Jordan. It would be a hell of a long way round."

Chase rose and took his customary seat on the windowsill, hands clasped between his knees. "What about the other brother?"

"I'm beginning to think he's not in on it, except for delivering the car to France. The journey to Bahrain seems to be a genuine business trip. He's been quite open about it."

"Better keep an eye on him."

"We've nobody in Bahrain. We'll have to do it through the Foreign Office, sir."

Chase nodded. "And it'll take time. I'll get that moving myself. What else?"

"France. I don't think he would have got a false passport.

It's not the sort of thing Giles Dunton would do. He's a grim, blunt man. He'll go at it doggedly, but without complications. After all, why shouldn't he be taking a holiday in his car? He just presents himself at frontiers as a tourist. You can get any necessary tourist visas as you go along. If I'm right, he's already out of France, but they'll have records of his entry and exit, and where he stayed."

"So?"

"What do I tell them, sir? I was wondering if you'd get through to Paris at a high level and indicate that it's only a routine inquiry at present, and we'll keep them informed if anything develops."

"Very well. You know whom to get in touch with?"

"I was thinking of Dassier."

"He'll do."

Back at his own desk, Kennard put through a call to a small office in the Douane headquarters building where Henri Dassier worked, the specialist in frontier movements.

"Henri? Harvey Kennard here. Yes, nice to talk again. You're well? Good. Yes, me too. Listen, Henri, we want tabs on Major Giles Rees Dunton. I'm pretty sure he entered France, possibly from Ireland, within the past week, maybe in the last three or four days, probably by air. He had a car waiting for him, an English car. I'll let you know the make and registration number as soon as I can. My guess is that he has already driven the car out of France, probably into Italy, but possibly through Switzerland or Germany, and there's a faint chance he may have shipped it over to Algeria, perhaps after crossing into Spain. Yes, you may well laugh. It's certainly vague. We don't want him picked up, but just to know where he is. By the way, he might be armed. May I leave it at that? Thanks, Henri, you are very understanding. Regards to Madame Dassier and little Marie. Thanks a lot."

When he had hung up, Kennard stared hard at the map. Suppose Dunton had started from Paris three days ago. He might easily drive four hundred miles a day. That would take him comfortably to the heel of Italy, or into Yugoslavia, or well into North Africa if ferry sailings fitted. Suppose he had been driving for only two days. . . . It was hopeless without more information. The bloody man might be anywhere.

He walked to Charing Cross and took the train home. He had phoned Sally as soon as he got back to London and she sounded amiable. All the same, he hesitated before climbing the stairs.

To his astonishment she greeted him lovingly. "I've been such a bitch to you, darling. Forgive me."

"Nothing to forgive."

"You were right about Maurice. I went to see the girl—she's a blowsy tart."

"How did you find her?"

"He has only one block of flats in Streatham, and she's the only singleton there. I watched her come out. No, I didn't say anything."

He saw that she was dressed up. "Let's go out to dinner," he proposed.

"No, I've a nice dinner for you."

She had, and a bottle of almost undrinkable Burgundy from the grocer; but he had plenty of scotch. Afterward she went docilely to bed. The moment he touched her she responded wildly. When it was over, she lay beside him, sobbing. He gently soothed her, stroked her naked back. He knew very well that, within a month or two, she would be hooking up with some other man if she could get one. It had happened so often before—unfaithfulness, repentance, eager loving, then boredom.

She had stopped sobbing and was tentatively fondling

him again. He did his best to make it, and at last succeeded, but more weakly. Then he could get some sleep.

§

The Foreign Office pulled its finger out more smartly than Kennard had expected. Chase told him that a fellow named James Crozier, on the staff of the Political Resident in Manama, had been ordered to watch Mark Dunton and to report any unusual activity, and particularly if he left Bahrain for anywhere else. His reports to the Foreign Office would be repeated to the department.

Dassier was slower. It was not until Sunday afternoon that he came through, rather faint on a poor line: "Harvey, there's something odd. There's a record of your man staying last Tuesday night at a small hotel in Paris, the Mercurieur. He left next morning in his car, which was delivered to the hotel garage on the twenty-fifth."

"Interesting," said Kennard, "but not all that odd."

"Ah, it is not that. There is no record of his entering France—none at all. We have gone back two weeks. Could it have been earlier?"

"No. That's certain."

"Then we have a flaw which I must seek out and remedy."

Kennard asked, rather more anxiously, "Any record of his leaving?"

"None as yet, although there is more inquiry to be made."

"By car," said Kennard. "I think he must have left by car."

"Not by any of the normal routes into Germany, Switzerland, or Italy. We have yet to complete the check on the frontiers with Belgium and Spain."

"I suppose there could be lesser roads along which he could be smuggled."

"Not easy," said Dassier. "Also, he has not left by air on any commercial route. Of course, it is possible, but difficult, to jump over a frontier from some remote place in a small airplane or helicopter."

Kennard groaned. "That I hadn't thought of."

He realized he must find out whether Dunton could pilot an aircraft. Until he knew that, he could scarcely ask Dassier to check on hired machines over the whole of France. Already the Frenchman sounded a little tired of the thing.

"Henri," said Kennard, "you don't know how grateful I am for your help."

"Is it truly something serious, my friend?"

"Frankly, I don't know. But it could be very serious indeed."

"Ah, then that is all I wish to know."

"Have you had time to check the Mediterranean ferries? Oh, but you can't have done. I am asking too much."

"We have checked them. He has not taken his car that way. There are still some other aspects of port records we must investigate, but it will not be possible until tomorrow. I shall telephone you if we find anything."

"Thank you, Henri. From the bottom of my heart."

"It is nothing, my friend."

Kennard went home wearily. Sally, bored with having been left for so long, was drinking gin, and it made her irritable. Placatory, Kennard himself fried bacon and eggs for supper.

§

After Kennard left, Helen Dunton began to worry out the implications. He could have meant only that, for reasons she did not know, it was suspected that Giles intended some violent revenge for his brother's death.

Was Mark involved?

She remembered uncomfortably the long evening of the funeral, when she had sat in the drawing room with Gwen and Jean, and the two men had not come from the table.

"What were you talking about for so long?" she asked Mark in the bedroom.

"Anthony," he replied abruptly.

She had not dreamed of anything to follow. But now she feared. Was Mark entangled? The question worried her far into the night. In the early hours she decided that, as soon as she decently could, she would ring Gwen. She might know something.

The bailiff answered her call. "But Mrs. Dunton isn't here. I thought you knew. She's on her way to visit her mother in America."

Helen put down the phone, dismayed. Giles must be putting himself at risk, and had placed his wife in refuge; she had not thought him so considerate.

What the risk was she did not try to guess. Only one alarm sounded. Mark. Was that why he had gone to Bahrain?

Later in the morning she rang Mr. Saunders, Mark's closest associate at the bank. "Mark's visit to Bahrain, Mr. Saunders—was it his idea?"

"I really don't know, Helen. These things come up at meetings and are tossed around."

"Have you heard from him?"

"We wouldn't expect to hear until he has something to report, and that could be several days, or perhaps weeks. Negotiations with Arabs take a long, long time. When he gets anything, he will no doubt work through Spooner and Grant—our corresponding agents for the Persian Gulf. Their head office is on Bahrain Island."

"Do you know where Mark is staying?"

"He said he'd fix himself up when he got there. There are

several new hotels in Manama—very luxurious, and very expensive. I expect Mark will get into one of the residency houses if he can, or stay with one of his contacts. This time of year, you need the best accommodation you can get. It's a shocking climate, real Gulf stuff, temperature well over 100, and humid as hell—though I suppose hell's really the reverse of humid."

She laughed dutifully. Mr. Saunders always expected appreciation of his wit.

"If you haven't heard from him yet, Helen, I shouldn't worry. He has scarcely arrived, and must be damn busy. I'll let you know directly we get word."

There seemed nothing more for her to do. She reproached herself for being a fidget. It was an understood thing that they were independent of each other. Not unfaithful, of course, though going to bed with somebody else was not ruled out; she simply had no wish to and neither, she felt sure, had he.

She spent an uneasy weekend. On Monday she cashed a check at the bank around the corner from her office, where she and Mark kept their household joint account. She asked the clerk for the account balance. To her astonishment, the slip of paper he passed to her read, "Nil balance."

She saw the bank manager behind the clerk and asked him if he could spare a moment. Of course.

"Something's wrong," she said, pushing the paper across his desk. "There ought to be well over £700."

The bank manager went to check, and returned to his office apologetic. "It was the clerk at fault. I'm so sorry. He gave you the balance on your husband's loan account, instead of on your joint current account. The correct balance on the latter is £748.75."

"But there's still something wrong," she protested. The

loan account was that on which Mark had raised the equity needed to buy their house. "The loan account is still overdrawn by something like £2,000."

"Until last week," said the bank manager, smiling. "Then Captain Dunton paid off the outstanding balance." He glanced at a note on his desk. "Precisely £2,136.50. He asked me to keep the account in being for a few weeks, in case he should want to reinstate some of the loan. I agreed, of course."

Helen stared at him, trying to take it in; trying not to admit to herself that she knew what it must mean.

She returned to her office and sat with an open manuscript, but not reading it. Mark must have got the money from Giles; he was rich enough. But he would surely not have paid it unless Mark made it a condition. Condition of what? That was the frightening question. Mark would not have borrowed to extinguish the loan unless he knew that he was taking a serious risk. So, if he were killed, she would be left the house unburdened by debt.

It was revenge for Anthony's death. It could be nothing else. Bu+ what revenge? Since it was to be in Bahrain, perhaps they intended to sabotage an oil well, or something of that kind. If it were not so wild, so desperate, it would seem childish. But men are viciously childish, she muttered to herself, particularly regimental men.

She shut the manuscript, put it into her desk drawer, and went to see her editorial director.

"I've had an air letter from Mark," she lied. "He's having a grand time and asks if I can get out there to join him. I've a fortnight's holiday due. May I take it now?"

"Of course. Buy your air tickets through the firm. We get a discount."

Later in the day his secretary came through. "I've booked

you on a BOAC flight to Bahrain from Heathrow at 09:10 hours on Thursday. That's the earliest it can be done."

Helen could only pray that she reached him before he acted. If she were with him, she knew she could stop him.

§

Kennard was nervously impatient, irascible. Already it was Tuesday, and he had nothing more to go on. Each day he talked to Dassier, but no trace had been found of Giles Dunton's departure from France. Yet it was impossible he should still be in that country. That did not make sense.

There had been nothing from Bahrain either.

"I'll nudge them," said Chase.

Next day he came through on the internal line. "You can't expect a man posted to Bahrain, in the hot season, to be brilliant . . ."

"Crozier, sir?"

"Yes. I got my chap at the Foreign Office to query him. He said he has nothing to report, because Captain Dunton hasn't yet arrived."

"And it didn't occur to him to tell us that!"

"Better find out what happened to him."

It was not a difficult inquiry. The airline had the record. Captain Dunton had decided, after the aircraft left London, to break his journey at Beirut. He was entitled to. The aircraft captain, as a formality, had radioed London for permission. There was no objection.

Kennard to Chase: "I talked on the phone to Miller in Lebanon, sir. Mark Dunton's there all right, quite openly. He has been holding meetings with Beirut businessmen and a few minor politicians. All perfectly normal for a banker."

"I suppose we're not up quite the wrong creek, Kennard?"

"How about the other brother, sir?"

"True. Anything on him?"

"Not yet."

But early that evening Dassier came through. "At last we have him. He left Marseilles on a holiday cruise in the Mediterranean, in a ship called the *Montélimar,* on Friday last, August 28. That is the reason we have been so long, my friend. Records for tourists on holiday cruises are separate from records of normal emigration. This is also something of which I must inquire, for the future."

"Does the ship make any calls?"

"At Naples, Piraeus, Beirut . . ."

"When does she reach Beirut?"

"She arrived this morning," said Dassier, "and will depart later tonight for Alexandria. After that, only Tunis, then home to Marseilles."

"Is it possible to reach the captain, to inquire . . .?"

"I have anticipated you, Harvey. Major Dunton took advantage of the line's excursion arrangements, to spend one month in the Middle East, visiting the ruins of ancient cities, and returning home on the line's next cruise ship. The excursionists used to visit also the shrines of the Holy Land, but no longer, of course."

"So?"

"So Major Dunton disembarked at Beirut shortly before noon today."

8

There were traps to be avoided, Giles knew, from the moment he came ashore; just as there had been a particular trap to avoid during the voyage in the *Montélimar*.

That had been the temptation to display too much interest in the violence boiling up in Jordan.

There were few references to it in the scrappy news bulletins which the radio operator typed out each morning and pinned on the ship's bulletin board. But there was a passenger, a middle-aged, stout Frenchman, M. Georges Patin, who enlarged on it all the time. He was an official returning to the French embassy in Amman. He carried with him a portable radio which he tuned to every news broadcast he could find on the scale; then discoursed to a small group of passengers in the forward saloon on the holocaust which would soon occur in Jordan.

On the second day Giles sat close to the Patin gathering during the drinking hour before dinner. He ventured to insert a comment in English.

"But surely," he asked, "haven't the guns been silent on

the Jordan frontier, as well as along the Suez Canal, since the cease-fire proposed by the Americans began?"

"It is not external warfare that Jordan must fear at this time, monsieur," said the stout Frenchman, courteously replying in English. "It is civil war. Do you realize that the leader of the Palestinians in Jordan, Yassir Arafat, has constructed a force of some twenty thousand guerrillas, well equipped with Russian arms, well trained, and now being supplied also by the Chinese, who are sending not only supplies of such weapons as mortars and rockets, but also military instructors into the big refugee camps?"

"Yassir Arafat," murmured Giles. "Yes, I have heard of him. Does he really control them all?"

M. Patin nodded sagely. "I assure you. He has worked for years, building his strength in the refugee camps where the Palestinians have lived in disgraceful conditions for a generation. That is the basic scandal, monsieur. That is what has enabled Arafat to form an army from a mob. And now that peace talks have started in New York between Israelis and Arabs, under the auspices of the Americans . . . You are American, monsieur?"

"No, English."

"Ah, English. Then you will have a more experienced view of the tragedies of the Near East."

Giles laughed. "Not I, I'm afraid. I'm simply a tourist, visiting Beirut because I have some cousins there. I hope to see some of the famous ruins in Lebanon, and perhaps to visit Damascus. But I shall certainly stay well clear of Jordan."

"You are wise, monsieur. There will be a cataclysm in that country. Much blood will flow. It cannot be long delayed. The Palestinians must strive to halt the peace talks, or surrender all hope of regaining Palestine. They will fight.

Arafat himself has said so. He said, only a few days ago, 'We shall turn Jordan into a graveyard.'"

"Has he the strength?"

"In actuality, no. The Jordan army, composed mostly of Bedouin, renowned fighting men, numbers twice as many soldiers as Arafat's guerrillas. But the army has been held back, by the King, and by the influence of President Nasser of Egypt. Arab must not fight Arab. A friend of mine saw an armored car driving through Amman with a woman's brassiere hanging from its gun muzzle. Its commander explained bitterly, 'We are all women now.'"

The little group of passengers around M. Patin smiled sympathetically, and murmured that humiliation was something that the military could never for long tolerate; and they gestured to the bar steward to bring three more glasses of Pernod, and a fresh bottle of light wine.

During the brief calls which the *Montélimar* made at Naples and then at Piraeus, Giles managed to get two-day-old copies of *The Times* and *Le Monde*. From these he learned how gravely the Jordan thing had deteriorated. Guerrillas were manning barricades in the streets of the capital, Amman. Armored brigades were said to be moving into position around the city, encircling Arafat's central forces. In the north, around the cities of Irbid, Ramtha, and Jerash, there was already a state of almost open war.

On the fifth evening M. Patin held a much larger audience in the saloon. His news was dramatic. All communication with Jordan had been cut. There were unconfirmed stories that King Hussein had been ambushed in his car as he was driving to Amman to meet his daughter, Princess Alia, returning from a visit to her mother, ex-Queen Dina, in Cairo. Some reports said the king had been killed, others that he had survived and his troops had turned their guns on the guerrilla quarters of Amman, and the slaughter had been terrible.

Giles sat in his cabin that night, musing, scowling. Ironic, he told himself grimly, if Arafat were to be killed in ordinary combat before he could reach him.

His thoughts were interrupted by a knock on the door. Shirle. He smiled and brought her in. On the second night of the voyage he had had to persuade her to his cabin for a repetition. On the third and fourth nights she came uninvited, but not unwelcome. Shirle's educational project, Giles thought with amusement, was progressing well. At first her very naiveté was the enticement. But in so short a time he had now markedly improved her mechanical techniques, and roused in her a smoldering interest, rather more than a faint glow of desire.

§

In the morning, as the *Montélimar* approached Beirut, M. Patin was out on deck, recounting to an even larger group of passengers the more reliable news he had now received. The king had escaped harm, and was safely back in his palace. The army had shelled sections of the city mercilessly. The toll was reported as twenty known dead, and fifty wounded, and probably as many again as yet unknown.

M. Patin spotted Giles as, hoisting his grip, he was making ready for the gangplank to the shore.

"Ah, M. Dunton, have you heard? In the north of Jordan there is already heavy fighting and the guerrillas are said to be gaining the day. If you are wise, you will not go near Jordan, or even into Syria."

Giles waved cheerful assent. "Have no fear, M. Patin. I am on holiday. I want nothing to do with fighting. You and I have seen enough of that in our time, eh? Thank you for the warning. I am grateful."

So with another wave he went ashore.

He had successfully avoided the trap on the journey, he told himself. But there were other traps to be avoided now that he had disembarked.

The first was the danger of compromising his role of tourist. On his disembarkation card he had given his Beirut address as the St. George's Hotel. He must register there, and stay for at least one night, therefore.

The second trap was the telephone. He could not be sure whether a record was kept of calls from his hotel room. He would use only public callboxes.

The third was not so much a trap as an embarrassment —Shirle. She came ashore in her gypsy-like costume, with a large aluminum-framed rucksack on her shoulders, and in her hand a paperback entitled *The Holy Land on Five Dollars a Day*. Not that she intended, she cheerfully informed him, to spend nearly as much as that.

She was a nuisance, of course, but Giles realized instantly that it would be dangerous to drop her abruptly. He had been rash, no doubt, to encumber himself with even a slight recognition risk. Had he known that she was to disembark at Beirut he would have left her alone, he tried to persuade himself; but then admitted that he would probably have taken her to bed anyway.

"If you're going to manage on less than five dollars a day," he said, "you'd better start with a good lunch."

So he took her in a taxi to the hotel, checked in her rucksack with the porter, and left her staring around with benign scorn while he registered.

"What a place to stay!" she declared. "All you'll meet here is Americans—and maybe a couple of British."

He laughed and propelled her with a pat on the bottom toward the dining room. "But I love Americans."

Over lunch she told him at length of her plans for touring the countryside. She would walk if need be, or thumb lifts, and find youth hostels or Y.W.'s to stay in, or, if not, the places recommended in her little guidebook.

"Be a bit careful," he advised. "This isn't America. There's a lot of violence around."

"In America too."

"It's much worse here. They're on the edge of war—I don't mean with Israel, though that also—but among themselves. Wild men are roaming around with guns, blazing off at random. Better be warned."

She would be all right, she cheerfully assured him. It would all be *fun*. She wanted to live the life of the people in any country she was in, not stick herself into some international hotel and the tourist groove. When they had finished lunch, how about going to his room to spend the afternoon in bed?

"Sorry," he told her. "I've appointments to see the tourist people."

Oh, well, there would be another time. When she had spent a couple of weeks in the Holy Land, she intended to thumb a lift through Turkey into Europe, and she'd be sure to get to Britain. Maybe they'd meet in London. Was he in the London telephone book?

"Yes," he lied. "Call me when you get there."

So after lunch he retrieved her rucksack, which she shrugged onto her shoulders as he led her out of the hotel.

"Goodbye, then," she said. "Thanks a lot. Be seeing you."

He waved as she turned away. He would take damn good care that she wouldn't be. He watched for a few moments as she walked leisurely off, the rucksack bobbing gently. Then he stepped back into the hotel, reclaimed his passport, and went to the American Express.

"Major Giles Dunton. There should be a message for me."

The clerk handed over an envelope. It contained only the address and telephone number of the hotel in which Mark was lodged. There was a phone booth from which he made the call. Captain Dunton was out; was there a message?

"Tell him the caller is at the St. George's Hotel."

"Your name, sir?"

"He'll know."

In spite of the heat he strolled into the town, gazing at the office blocks, the smart little chichi shops, and the limousines gliding through the streets with shirtsleeved chauffeurs and, in the back, small stout men in expensive suits. There were still isolated villas, traces of the provincial Beirut he had known a couple of decades earlier, but most had vanished into grandiose, gaudy buildings shading the staring sun from street canyons where dubious deals running into millions were negotiated with eastern deviousness—clip city.

Back in his hotel room he took a shower to wash off the sweat, put on a thin shirt and slacks, and lay on the bed. He switched on the wall radio. An announcer was just finishing in French. Then came tinny bells, the whine of Arab music, and a voice in Arabic. Giles noted with satisfaction that he could still get almost all of it. Jordan dominated the bulletin. The Palestine Liberation Organization denied there had been an attempt on the life of King Hussein; it was a fake, to cover the crime of shelling the poorer quarters of Amman. From Baghdad the Iraqi government was threatening to order its twelve thousand troops in Jordan to turn on the Jordan army. The U.S. President declared he was not proposing to send American troops as a peace-keeping force. Two Lebanese and an American were up in a London police court after a police raid had found machine guns and ammunition in suitcases in the Hilton's left-luggage store.

Giles switched off. He wanted to sleep.

He was wakened by the telephone. "A gentleman to see you, sir."

"Send him up."

Mark was already brown-skinned and looked happy. "Going well? Any snags?"

Giles told him of the arrival at Belfast, and then at Dublin, of the man from Anthony's department, Harvey Kennard. "He was at the funeral."

"You think he was onto you? But what is there, so far, to be onto? Why were you in Ireland?"

Giles told him of the link between the antiterrorist groups in Belfast and Lebanon. "The Irish are being run by Bruce Oliphant."

"Do you think Anthony's people know he's your friend?"

"Possibly. But that doesn't mean Kennard was in Ireland looking for me. Bruce was certain he must be, but I think he was there on their account. Either way, it no longer matters. I gave him the slip in Dublin, at the airport."

"He was there," Mark asked, "at the same time as you? Then he must be onto you."

Giles shrugged. "I think not. But anyway, he can't trace me from then on. How about you? Is your end fixed?"

"I have a self-drive car—it's outside now. I've met several banking contacts, rather profitably as it happens. I can go home with a substantial amount of new business to account for this trip. I ought to phone London, but—"

"Don't," his brother ordered. "You're supposed to be in Bahrain."

"They may have found out by now that I'm not."

"I doubt it. If they had, they'd have been in touch with you here."

Mark agreed. "I've put round the tale that I'm planning a motoring tour of the north, and possibly into Syria. What's next?"

"The most valuable thing I got from Bruce Oliphant," said Giles, "was a contact and a safe house here in Beirut, and a promise I'll be passed on to a similar contact in Jordan."

"And the weapons, and anything else we need?"

"I hope so. Tonight I have to stay here, to substantiate the entry documents. Tomorrow I'll pay in advance, keep the room on, and tell them I'm making a tourist trip and will be back in a few days. You do the same at your hotel. By the time they even begin to wonder, we'll be clear of Lebanon. When we return I'll reregister, apologize for not letting them know, but the tourist attractions led me farther and for longer than I intended. Then I wait here for the next cruise sailing. I've got a month."

He explained the arrangement.

"It's not a bad reentry," Mark agreed. "I suppose I simply fly on to Bahrain."

"Certainly. Now, tomorrow I'll take a taxi to meet you. Where?"

"The railway station?"

"Fine. Park your car there at eleven hundred hours. I'll pay off the taxi, wait until it has driven off, then join you. You can drop me at the safe house."

"Where's that?"

"Tell you tomorrow. You'd better leave now."

§

He identified Mark's parked car as the taxi drove up to the station. The taxi, getting into line, was hired within minutes. Carrying his grip, Giles walked behind the parked cars and slid unobtrusively into the rear seat of his brother's. "Let's start."

"Where to?"

Giles gave him Louis Mouzouri's address. "Know it?"

"A pleasant spot, south of the town."

As they came away from the main promontory on which Beirut is built, Giles began to relax. They were soon driving along the coast road, lined with hibiscus, acacia, huge sunflowers, and gray-green eucalyptus; past villas hidden in flower-smothered gardens; through olive groves. On the right lay blue-water bays and small sandy coves. Above them on the left hung the mountains, dominated by Sannine, still, as Giles remembered her, snow-capped.

As he leaned back in the seat behind his brother, feeling uneasily guilty at enjoying all this, the driving mirror was in his line of vision. He noticed there was a car traveling at quite a distance behind them, not attempting to catch up. A blue Citroën.

He watched it for several minutes, then said to Mark, "Do you see the blue Citroën in your mirror? I think it's following us."

Mark glanced at the mirror. "It's been there for some time."

"Have you seen it following you before today?"

"Can't say I have. But then, I haven't been looking. It never occurred to me there could be anybody interested."

They both kept a watch on the mirror. The blue Citroën kept steadily at about the same distance. Giles memorized its registration number.

"What we want," he said, "is a road turning off into the mountains. Not too much of a side road, but twisting and turning."

"About a mile ahead."

Mark took the turning suddenly, without warning.

"I'll watch the mirror," said Giles.

Shortly after, the blue Citroën turned the same corner, keeping the same distance. Giles could make out only a driver in it, nobody else.

"It's turned after us," he reported. "We need to lose it."

Mark chose the place carefully. At every left-handed curve he was for less than a minute out of sight of the car behind. Immediately around one curve he spurted, turned into the entrance to a circular drive in front of a villa, pulled up in the shelter of bushes.

The blue Citroën sped past.

There was a face at one of the windows of the villa.

"Better get out," said Mark.

"Give it a minute, so that the car gets round the next curve."

The door of the villa opened and a man emerged.

"Right," said Giles. "Let's go."

Mark spun the car angrily on the gravel, past the astonished man, and squealed out of the entrance onto the road.

"Fast as you can, the way we came," Giles ordered.

If the Citroën were following, he calculated that the driver would suspect the trick after another couple of miles and come hurrying back to look for them.

When they were once more on the coast road, he asked Mark, "How far to the house?"

"About a mile, perhaps a little more. It's a big villa standing back from the road, on the left, up a small hill."

"When you get there, let me off. Then drive on fast. Can you take a circle route back into Beirut? Good. Get back to your hotel and wait for a message. We'd better have a key. My message, even if it's me on the phone, will start with the words, 'The major says,' and your reply will start, 'The captain answers.'"

Mark pulled the car up. "Here. That villa up there to the left."

Giles grabbed his grip and stepped out. As the car drove away, he dropped behind a clump of tamarisk at the roadside. It took five minutes' waiting, then the blue Citroën went by, traveling too fast for him to see much of the driver.

So it was positive. But who? He shook his head. No time for that now.

A sandy drive turned off the road toward the wide, tall, wrought-iron gates that pierced the high cement wall around the grounds of the villa. The gates were locked, but an entry phone was fastened to one of the stone pillars. When he pressed, a woman's voice inquired in French who was there, please?

He gave his name, then answered in French that he had come to see M. Mouzouri, with an introduction from a friend in Ireland.

There was a pause. Then a man's voice asked, in English, "Who is this friend, please?"

"Major Bruce Oliphant."

"And your name, please?"

"Giles Dunton."

The iron gates buzzed and loosened.

"Come in, please, Major Dunton. Come to the villa entrance, please."

The gates closed softly behind him, locking.

The drive climbed through a huge, beautifully tended garden with bowers, a rose walk, a gazebo slenderly wrought of iron, white-painted. The villa itself was also white, with rose-pink window shutters, a flat roof. Plants bloomed all around it and over its walls.

A young man stood at the open front door. "M. Mouzouri

has been telephoned and will arrive soon from his office. I am a secretary. Come in, please."

The inside of the house was sumptuous—marble floors, heavy furnishings, a few modern landscape oils that Giles guessed would be valuable. The main room opened onto a wide terrace under a brilliant orange awning, overlooking the garden at the rear. The terrace was equipped with white garden chairs, glass-topped tables, a canopied swing seat from which a girl rose to greet him; brunette, slender but rather short, with delicate features.

"Madame Mouzouri?"

"No, I am the daughter. My father is a widower. Perhaps you should know that my mother died as your brother. No, not a bomb. In a car that was ambushed, in mistake for another, on the road from Damascus."

Giles murmured regrets.

"It is three years now," she answered. "But it is still better not to speak of it to my father. Now, Major Dunton, you will drink something? A dry martini?"

She mixed it from a trolley of drinks against the terrace wall; then sat beside him, carefully talking commonplaces until her father came.

He also was rather short, slightly plump, immaculate; his manner friendly, but grave. His daughter poured him an iced fruit juice, and they sat talking meaninglessly about the loveliness of the garden, his journey, the changes he saw in Beirut since the late 1940's.

But there was one piece of information Giles must offer immediately. "You know my brother is already in Beirut? Ah, yes, you will have inquired when Bruce Oliphant told you of us. My brother drove me here in a car he has hired. We were followed."

Mouzouri showed anxiety only by a lifted eyebrow. Giles

told him of the blue Citroën and gave him the registration number, which he noted in a small, gold-cased jotting pad he took from his breast pocket.

"We shook him off for long enough for Mark to drop me here undetected," Giles reassured him. "But the fact of being followed, when I thought my whereabouts were unknown to anybody who matters, is disturbing. It would be good to know who the pursuer is."

Mouzouri inclined his head. He pressed a bell and gave his secretary the sheet from the jotting pad. "Telephone Solzeen to find out, quickly, who is the owner of that car."

The lunch was served on the terrace by a dark-skinned man in jibbal and fez. Mouzouri himself poured the wine, white, cool, a little too sweet. At the end of the meal the servant brought a tray of thick black coffee which Mouzouri's daughter dispensed from the beaten brass jugs; then excused herself, and went.

Mouzouri turned to Giles. "What do you want of me? I already know from Major Oliphant your purpose."

"Which you approve?"

Mouzouri gravely inclined his head. "Nobody can deny that the Palestinian Arabs have been shamefully treated. Nobody could fail to understand the anger and desperation which have driven a naturally indolent, kindly people to acts of terrorism. But they must cease. Our corner of the world cannot continue forever in armed conflict. The insane acts of terrorism must be halted."

"It can be done only by individuals."

"I agree. Governments are helpless—more bombs, more hijacked aircraft, more hostages. So it must be done by individuals. But you set yourself a difficult target, Major Dunton."

Speaking in Arabic, Giles said, "I have, as you can hear,

this advantage, at least. I have passed as an Arab years ago. Tell me, can I still?"

Mouzouri replied, also in Arabic, "I think you may. You must say you are from Palestine. There are traces of that country in your speech. Very well then, what do you want from me?"

"Here in Beirut, cover for our tracks—my brother's and mine. We are telling our hotels we are touring by car, and to keep our rooms. Is it possible to arrange that the hotels' reports to the police are mislaid for a week or so?"

"It is easy."

"I need to be able to change sterling, without official record, into Jordan dinars."

"There is no difficulty. Give my secretary the sterling."

"I need Arab clothing for us both, and two revolvers, preferably Smith and Wesson forty-fives. We need to leave our hired car in Lebanon, near the Syrian frontier, and substitute transport of the kind that guerrillas are using."

"I will give you instructions before you leave."

"In Jordan we need a safe house and a contact who will furnish us with weapons."

Mouzouri assented again. He would supply a name before Major Dunton departed.

He was interrupted by his secretary, who brought in a folded piece of paper. Mouzouri read it, gestured to the secretary to leave, then told Giles, "The car that followed you belongs to an Englishman, Gregory Miller. He is an employee of your Middle East Regional Information Office, housed in the British embassy in Beirut. We know him to be a British agent."

9

Early that evening Harvey Kennard arrived at Beirut airport. The heat struck up from the concrete. As the aircraft taxied in, he was already sweating in the lightest suit he had grabbed from his wardrobe. Sally had bitched, naturally, but he was experienced in fending that off.

While he was waiting for his suitcase to come through, he saw Gregory Miller in the small crowd of greeters. He was annoyed at the risk of being compromised, but relieved at the promise of comfort.

"It would have been better if you had let me come in by myself as a tourist," he told Miller when they were driving away from the airport.

Miller laughed. He was young, pansy-looking, wavy fair hair; inexperienced, Kennard guessed, but his record was surprisingly tough.

"It wouldn't have made the least difference," he assured Kennard. "In this town, both sides would have spotted you within twenty-four hours. So I've booked you a room in the embassy annex, which has a back door into a side street that isn't often watched."

Kennard grunted. "I take it you've located the elder brother and have him under surveillance."

"I had until this morning," Miller admitted. "But I've lost him." He related how he had been given the slip. "Sorry about that."

Kennard grunted again. This was the man with whom he would have to work.

"Mark Dunton's back at his hotel, a small one in a suburb where quite a lot of bankers and general moneylenders hang out. I've a man watching."

"Any idea where Giles is cached?" asked Kennard.

"None, I'm afraid, except that it's somewhere south of the city. But we'll pick him up the moment he makes contact with his brother."

Maybe, Kennard thought to himself. Giles Dunton was beginning to impress him. But he said nothing.

"On the way to the annex," suggested Miller, "we'd better stop off to buy you lighter clothes. You must be broiled in that rig. The shops in the suqs stay open to all hours."

And when he was installed in the annex, had taken a shower and dressed in a light suit, Kennard felt human again.

Miller picked him up, to drive him to a small, special place to eat. "Relax," Miller urged him. "There's nothing you can do tonight. Mark is in his hotel, entertaining three of his financial chums and their wives to dinner. The brothers won't move until they join."

"I'm not so sure. Giles could have gone on and left Mark as a blind."

"Giles still has his room at the St. George's."

"Doesn't mean a thing."

They ate in one of several small bowers in the garden at the rear. The young crescent of the moon was just setting, leaving the purple sky brilliant with stars. They drank arrack with the mezzeh, dipping pieces of flat Arab bread into a rough-textured paste (baked eggplants mashed with lemon juice and garlic, Miller informed him), and picked at the clumps of raw vegetables and little hot peppers. For the main dish Miller recommended mousakhan—"Chicken split open on a round of Arab bread, sprinkled with red sumac berries, and grilled under charcoal. You'll like it." A rather heavy, sweet wine went with the dish. Afterward Kennard waved away sweetmeats and took only a slice of white goat's-milk cheese. He belched comfortably and leaned back in his chair. "Time I got posted away from Whitehall into the field."

He could have done without talk of the Duntons that evening. But Miller asked, "Have you any idea what they plan?"

"My guess is that they aim to avenge their brother's death by a political assassination."

"Here in Beirut?"

"No. What they're after is headlines, to discourage others. I reckon they'll go for the top. Arafat seems the most likely."

"Strewth! That'd put the camel turd, as they say, into the spiced mutton broth. But, man, they'd never get near him. He moves inside a shell of gunmen."

"Don't underestimate Giles Dunton," stressed Kennard. He told of the Arab-pose possibility. "And he and his brother are both highly trained and tough fighting men, a quality the El Fatah hysterics have never met."

"Arafat fought against the British in the Suez Canal thing," Miller reminded him. "A demolition officer in the Egyptian army at Port Said."

"It didn't last long enough for the lads even to get their

knees brown before Eden lost his nerve and pulled them back. Don't mistake, Miller. Men like the Duntons might well get close enough to kill Arafat. And what would that do?"

"Set the whole Middle East thing on fire again. Sure, they've got to be stopped."

"It's my guess," Kennard told him, "that they'll be moving tomorrow. They've obviously got good contacts here, so they probably know it was you tailing them this morning, and that I've arrived. They both know me."

"Because of Anthony? Yes, of course."

"Can you get a solid, fast car?" asked Kennard, adding with a grin, "Not a blue Citroën."

"I can borrow a Rover 3500 from the stable."

"Fine. You and I will stand by from first light, to follow Mark if he moves. This time he mustn't shake you."

"This time," Miller promised, "he won't."

§

"Last night," Louis Mouzouri told Giles, "the man who followed you in the blue Citroën, Gregory Miller, went to the airport to meet an Englishman from London. He is staying at the embassy. A Mr. Kennard. I see that you know him."

"He is in the security department where my brother Anthony worked. He was at the funeral."

"Why should Mr. Kennard be here?"

"I don't know. But I have to admit now that he is trying to find me—now that he is in Beirut."

The Lebanese said softly, "Either you must abandon your plan or you must start today."

"It is not to be abandoned."

Mouzouri lifted from a side table a thin leather wallet.

"Here is the exchange for your sterling. You and your brother must set out from Beirut in his car this morning. You will certainly be followed. Do not concern yourself with that. Do you know the town of Zahle?"

"On the Damascus road, about thirty miles east of here. I have driven through it, but I do not know it."

"On the outskirts there is a big garage for gasoline, with the name Zinga and a large white crescent on its sign. Drive directly into the workshop that lies behind and ask for the manager. His name is Sanari. He will provide what you want, and keep the hired car hidden until you return."

"Thank you. I'm grateful."

"Do not try to cross the frontier into Syria by any of the usual routes. Your English friends may have alerted the Lebanese authorities. Drive south toward the town of Rachaya. The El Fatah guerrillas hold most of the mountains around there. Units of our army still hold some of the old French forts, and there is occasional fighting. But the government no longer controls the south. East of Rachaya are rough tracks by which you can cross the mountains into Syria. You will have to find them for yourself, Major. I do not know exactly where the guerrillas may be." He smiled. "As you say, I think you must then play by your ear."

"And when we reach Jordan?"

"In a valley between the Syrian frontier and the north Jordan town of Jerash is a farm called Qasr el Sa'an—once there was a Crusader castle there. It is owned by Colonel Abdul Zouqa, formerly a soldier, then a palace official, now elderly and thought to be retired. He will expect you."

Giles asked, "Can you send a messenger to my brother at his hotel? Thank you. And if I make a rendezvous at the railway station, can you get us away in his car unhindered?"

"It can be arranged."

"Then the message is, 'The major says today, same place, same time. Acknowledge.' The exact words are important. And I shall need to be at the station at 10:55 hours exactly."

The Lebanese nodded and left the room.

Giles got his things into his grip, then waited, staring out of the window at the garden, the last peaceful thing he would see for, say, a week. Swiftly in, sharp assault, swift retreat. He would leave it to Mouzouri to arrange the publicity after; an announcement to the press that it was reprisal for terrorism in Europe by Palestinian murderers, and there would be further reprisals against Palestinian leaders for any new slaughter.

A while later Mouzouri's secretary came in.

"There is an answer, sir, which M. Mouzouri told me to deliver to you in exact words. It is, 'The captain answers, timing agreed.'"

"Thank you."

"M. Mouzouri also instructed me to say that at ten o'clock there will be a car waiting for you in the courtyard behind the villa. It is now only five minutes before ten o'clock."

"Let's go," said Giles, following him, taking a last hard look at the garden before he turned from the window.

§

It was 10:35 when word was phoned to Miller's office that Mark Dunton was moving. "He has put a case into his car as though he's making a trip, and is just starting in the direction of the town center. Fred's following."

Miller looked at Kennard. "Communications are the snag."

Kennard nodded. "But it's not a huge town. Let's get going."

As he drove, Miller said, "We've got to gamble on a guess. Yesterday Mark picked up his brother at the railway station. It's an easy place for a man to get from one car to another without being noticed."

"Surely they wouldn't use the same place twice."

"If not, where do we go?"

"Try it," said Kennard.

As they neared the station, Miller swung to the roadside and halted. "We guessed right. My man's car is parked just ahead."

He got out, lit a cigarette, walked slowly forward, had a word with the man in the car, and returned.

"Mark has his car parked round the next bend. My man can just see its rear fender." He started the motor. "We'd better get ahead of him, so that he's covered whichever way he moves."

But already the action was starting. Mark Dunton's car, with Giles in the rear seat, was heading back past them.

It was too narrow for Miller to circle. As he went forward to find a wider space, Kennard looked back and muttered, "They've snookered your man."

A battered taxi had pulled up alongside the tail car, and an elderly passenger was slowly emerging. Miller's man, leaning from his car, was shouting angrily to the taxi to get out of the way. The taxi driver, turning from his fare, began to shout angrily back. A traffic cop on a motorcycle was moving in from the distance. Neat, thought Kennard. Damn neat.

Miller swung his car into a turn.

"Take it slowly," Kennard warned. "I don't think they've spotted us yet. Don't attract them."

Whoever had planned it had completely blocked the car that had been tailing Mark Dunton. But he seemed not to have reckoned on a second pursuit car. Nevertheless,

Kennard was uneasy. It seemed unlikely that contingency had been overlooked. As they passed the taxi, the driver gesticulating wildly to the traffic cop who had just arrived, he saw another man beyond, in white slacks and blue shirt, staring at him as Miller gradually accelerated. Then the man turned and ran for a telephone booth.

Kennard grunted and straightened himself in the seat beside Miller. "Any idea where Dunton has gone?"

"Looks as though he's taking the main way out to the Damascus road. If I go a little faster, I can get continual sight of him."

As they came clear of the city Miller slowed to increase the distance between the two cars. Even so, Kennard felt sure the Duntons must realize they were being followed, or soon would, for there was little other traffic; a few limousines traveling fast, an overladen country bus, several cyclists, a peasant with a panniered donkey.

Kennard was trying to reckon the odds against making his play now. As though reading his thoughts, Miller said, "I could get ahead, cut in and force them off the road."

"Do you carry a gun?"

"No," said Miller cheerfully. "His Excellency's strict orders. No British official, etc. . . ."

So it was no good, Kennard reasoned. He himself had been forced, by airport security against hijackers, to travel unarmed.

"Too risky," he said. "Wait until they reach the frontier. We can stop them there. But don't lose them."

"Not to worry. We must have twice the speed of their hired jalopy."

They were out on the plain now, traveling through olive groves, grain fields, orchards; the mountains stood back on either side from this road.

From far behind came a ragged burst of gunfire. Kennard jerked up hastily.

Miller laughed. "It'll be a jeepload of fedayin. They're always trigger-happy, but it's usually firing into the air—just *joie de vivre*."

"Hope you're right," Kennard murmured.

Looking back, he could now see a jeep shuddering forward with a long plume of dust. As it neared, he could make out half a dozen Arabs, checkered headdresses bound with knotted cord, khaki shirts slanted with bandoliers, rifles and machine guns waving boisterously in the air and now and then firing.

Miller himself was looking worried now. "Shall I run for it? They couldn't keep up."

"No good. We'd simply be driven past the Duntons. Better slow to let them pass—if they're going to."

Miller glanced doubtfully, pulled well in to the side of the road, began to slow.

The jeep went roaring past, the Arabs shouting and laughing and waving their guns.

The dust cloud rolled over. The shots came through it.

Miller held the car as it slid crazily over the road, shuddering and swinging, pulling upon a sandy verge at right angles to the roadway.

He got out and walked to the front of the car, then gazed after the speeding dust plume.

Miller came back to the car door.

"They got both our front tires. We've only one spare."

§

As the jeep passed the Duntons' car, two Arabs standing up in the back clinging to the struts of the hood shouted cheerfully and loosed off a salvo into the air. Then the jeep swung right into a rutted side road, bumping through olive groves.

Mark grinned. "Your chum certainly has this place organized."

Giles said, "Better step on it. If they get to a phone they might bring the police in now. They know the road we're on."

"Could they possibly?"

"Through the embassy. Some faked-up excuse of finding two British tourists for whom there was an urgent message from England. How far to Zahle?"

"About fifteen miles."

Mark coaxed the hired car to its maximum, but he could not get the needle much past the one-hundred-kilometer mark. "If I push her any more she might bust something."

Ten minutes later Giles told him he would have to. "Listen."

Distantly behind them sounded the purr of a motorcycle.

Mark pushed his foot down flat. The old car complained, but the needle crept to 113. "She won't take any more."

"The town must be close now," said Giles, peering forward. "A big gasoline station, Zinga, and a white crescent on the sign." Then, a few minutes later, "There it is. Ease down, man. Straight into the workshop behind."

Mark was doubtful of the brakes. But, screaming, they slowed the thing sufficiently for him to swivel onto the garage forecourt, then ease the car through the large doors of the workshop.

As he cut the engine, there came the growl of a motorcycle passing along the road outside.

A mechanic working on a jacked-up Ford looked at them once, then took no further notice. A thick-set, black-haired man came out from a small office behind a glass window at one end of the workshop. He crossed to the internal wall and swung open what had seemed a wooden section. Beyond it descended a concrete ramp. The man gestured. Mark drove the car gently down into a pillared cellar. The door closed, and the dark man, switching on dim electric lighting, followed the car."

"M. Sanari?"

"Yes. You must not lose time." He pointed to a battered jeep standing by the wall. "That is for you. It looks worn, but is good inside. The garments you asked for are there. Put your other clothes in a case in your car. It will be here when you return." He started back up the ramp. "Press that bell when you are ready to go. The upstairs door will be open. Drive away without talk. Turn to the left, then to the left once more, a small road. It will take you outside Zahle. I have marked the road on a map. It is in the jeep."

"And the revolvers?" asked Giles.

"Also."

Giles sorted out the clothing piled in the jeep—ragged pants, thick brown sweaters, stained olive-green field jackets, black-and-white-checkered head scarves, and knotted black ropes with which to fasten them. He nodded approval; virtually the unofficial uniform of El Fatah guerrillas.

The revolvers were holstered onto leather belts. On the floor of the jeep stood a wooden box filled with shells. The map lay on the dashboard shelf. Mark opened another box in the rear of the vehicle; jerrycans of water, a skin of wine, packets of food, a flashlight, a compass, knives.

"Strip right out," ordered Giles. "Take nothing we came with."

"Underpants?"

"No. But better keep our dark glasses, and the flask of whiskey for emergencies."

Mark grimaced and began to strip.

The jeep started at a touch, purring reassuringly. Giles pressed the bell and climbed into the passenger seat. The door was open at the top of the ramp. There was no other traffic when they emerged onto the road, turning left, then left again onto a rough road piercing olive groves and fields of barley under date palms and apricot trees. The going was heavy, the jeep lurching, pitching. Giles clung with one hand to the strut of the torn canvas canopy, and with the other held the folded map on his knees.

"Once we're round Zahle we come out again onto the Damascus road. We stay on that, except for a detour marked round the next town, Shtora, until we branch right in the direction of Merj Uyun. That will still be a main road, but we get off it somewhere near Rachaya and work our way east over the mountains. Further south we'd risk running into the Israelis—they're as far into Syria as the slopes of Mount Hermon."

The heat by now was intense. The torn canopy gave scant protection. But once they had clambered out again onto the highway, it began to ascend the Anti-Lebanon range, gaining with altitude some relief. Higher up, however, the mountains became bare. There was no wind. The pressure of sun glare was intense; without the Arab headdresses it would have been intolerable.

After about twenty miles Giles said, "We must turn soon."

Almost immediately, as though in confirmation, a tattoo of rifle shots sounded distantly among the peaks.

"That side road to the left, to Rachaya?" asked Mark.

Giles nodded, and he swung onto it.

§

On the highway there had been a few cars. On this road there was nothing. The villages through which it ran seemed asleep in the sun, deserted; but occasionally there was a shawled figure turning into a doorway; or a face seen dimly through a dark window; and in the dust at the roadside yellow or brown mangy dogs raised their heads, then drooped again into silence.

The firing was louder now. As they neared Rachaya, Giles gestured to Mark to halt. A village lay in a small valley. Clustered around its entrance were a dozen jeeps, a few Arabs crouching or lying at the roadside near them, weapons slung over their shoulders.

"Light automatics," said Mark softly, "so far as I can make out."

Giles agreed. "Russian for sure. Which will make them Palestinians."

"The firing's just beyond."

A salvo pinpointed it. Beyond the houses rose a steep hill with an old French fort at the summit. The shots came from the fort. No men could be seen; they must be firing through the ancient arrow slits. Then Giles made out their targets. Straggling across the slope below the fort stretched a line of guerrillas, most in what cover the mountain scrub provided, a few prostrate in the open, legs twisted, arms spread, casualties. From the bushes came sporadic return fire.

"Lebanese troops in the fort," murmured Mark. "Should be impregnable—by daylight, anyhow."

Giles was gazing around the mountain slopes.

"Will the jeep take that track?" he asked, pointing.

It was narrow, encroached upon by scrub. It seemed roughly to follow the contour around the side of the nearest peak, hidden from the combat.

Mark said, "I think it'll go."

It was uncomfortable, but possible. Farther ahead, indeed, the track broadened. But then came an unpleasant stretch, very narrow, on the lip of a thousand-foot drop.

Muttering to himself, Mark took it gingerly, hesitant at every shift and slide of stones beneath his wheels. When the track at last turned aside from the precipice, he exhaled gratefully. "We'll find some other route back."

Now the track climbed steeply. But though the jeep looked decrepit, it could take it. The engine was finely tuned, and the tires new.

The apex of the track was not far from the peak; thence it dropped away sharply and could be seen below to turn along a lonely valley.

"The firing's not far on the other side," said Giles. "Let's climb to the top and have a look."

Mark halted the jeep in the shelter of a bush. The two of them scrambled up the stony, rock-strewn slope. At the top was a large boulder behind which they could lie, to peer down the far side.

They were slightly above and to the right of the fort. The guerrillas could not be made out on the slope below it. But then two of them broke cover and scrambled a few yards higher; a crackle of shots, and one fell.

"No covering fire, no diversion," murmured Mark. "Not the most highly trained of soldiers."

"Brave men, though." Giles had shifted his position so that he could look down the slope on the other shoulder of the mountain. He gestured to Mark. "Quietly."

Not more than five hundred feet below, hidden from the fort by the shoulder, a small convoy of five jeeps was making its way along a narrow track toward a group of guerrillas around the mouth of a cave. When the convoy halted, men leaped from the two leading and the two following vehicles, automatics swinging from their shoulders, to form a loose ring around the center jeep.

In this there was only one man. He climbed from the

driving seat and walked toward the cave, the waiting guerrillas waving joyfully, flocking toward him. The ring of machine-gunners from the four other jeeps moved slowly forward as the man in the center moved. He was short, stubby, a belt of pistols and cartridges hanging against a protuberant belly. His eyes were hidden by thick dark glasses. He wore the olive-green field jacket and the checkered headdress of the Arab guerrillas. His own machine gun was slung across his left arm.

"Arafat?" whispered Mark.

"It could be. He could have come across the mountains to meet his men fighting here."

The enlarged group was now moving slowly away along a footpath toward the ridge of the shoulder, doubtless to an observation point.

"If only we had rifles," said Mark regretfully.

"Talk sense. Even if we had rifles, we're not sure it's the right man. Even if it were, how would we get away? We're on a mountain we don't know, following tracks that aren't mapped and could lead anywhere—or, as dead ends, nowhere. You're forgetting the textbooks. Never improvise. Let's get back to the jeep. If that bunch is returning into Syria over these mountains, we'd better get ahead of them as soon as we can."

10

Her vacation from college was proving all that Shirle had hoped; in particular, she was keeping well out of the tourist groove and meeting people of the country.

The first she met was a dark, handsome young Lebanese whose given name she later learned to be Nasib; she never did, as it happened, come to know his family name. She met him on the beach of a small cove south of Beirut onto which she had turned for a swim. As she emerged from the lukewarm sea, there was this dark, handsome young man, dressed in negligible swimming trunks, squatting by the side of her pile of clothes and rucksack. "Hi," she said. "Hi," he replied. "Oh dandy," she said, "you speak English."

Well, they lay side by side on the beach for a while, and Nasib told her how he was having a week's vacation from the business house belonging to his father, and was spending most of it on the beach; he could, as a matter of fact, speak quite good English. But the sun was too hot to permit lying for long on a beach. She would blister, Nasib told her. Then he told her about the small hut belonging to his father at the head of the cove, which Nasib was using as a beach residence so that he could thoroughly enjoy his vacation. It was much pleasanter in the beach hut and, once Nasib had pulled the thin curtain across the entrance, quite private.

Later, when it was evening, Nasib lit a small oil lamp and produced food which he cooked on a small oil stove; and a bottle of thin wine. As they were eating it, Shirle began to giggle. Nasib asked what was so funny, and she searched in her rucksack for her guidebook and handed it to him. She said, laughing, that so far she was seeing the Holy Land, and having a fine time, on less than fifty cents a day. So Nasib laughed too and asked her where she was going to sleep that night, why not in his beach hut? Shirle said that was very kind and considerate of him, and she accepted with pleasure, and they spent the night very comfortably.

Early in the morning Shirle crossed the beach for another swim. Since there was nobody about she did not bother about her swimsuit. When Nasib, wakened by her departure, saw her crossing the beach, he went hurrying after her, and they had an enjoyable and leisurely swim together. Back in the beach hut Nasib got the little oil stove going and made coffee. Then he asked her what she would like to do with the day. He was still on vacation from his father's business, and he had one of his father's cars to use (his father had five cars), so he would take her wherever she wanted to go. So Shirle said she had always wanted to see Damascus. Nasib hesitated for a moment, because he was feeling to a certain extent tired. But then he said okay, and they got dressed and locked up the beach hut and slung Shirle's rucksack in the back of Nasib's father's car, and drove over the mountains to Damascus. Shirle was both ecstatic and peacefully happy.

With Damascus she was enchanted; all those lovely runnels and stone troughs and pools of running water, and all those pretty fountains! She consulted her guidebook, which took a view of the Holy Land generous enough to include Damascus, and led Nasib firmly on foot along one of the avenues leading to the Great Mosque, which, unfortunately, for reasons that were not clear to her, she was not permitted to enter. So then she plunged into a vigorous tour of the suqs, with Nasib following, and lagging a little now and then. She stared with delight at the fortune-tellers, the public scribes, the stalls selling bridles and harness and camel gear. "Oh, wow!" she exclaimed to Nasib. "Saddles for a camel! Isn't that cute?" Nasib nodded, but a shade wearily. So then she passed on to a thorough inspection of the goldsmiths' and silversmiths' booths, and the sherbet seller in his red-and-white skirt dispensing the stuff from a brass ewer, and the sweetmeat stalls, and the stalls piled with crystallized fruits, and much, much more. Nasib persuaded her to sit for a while outside a café, in the shade of a walnut tree, while they ate a spicy meat dish for lunch, followed by sugared fruit. But then she led him on again, indefatigably. In midafternoon Nasib said it was time to start back for Beirut. But Shirle protested there was much more to see. Nasib, who now had a headache, declared irritably that he was driving back to Beirut right away, and she was welcome to come or stay behind, just as she liked. Shirle decided she would stay behind. "There'll probably be a Y.W.," she told him, "or a youth hostel, or anyhow a rest house." So Nasib said goodbye and went off to find his car, not even looking back to wave to her.

§

There was in fact a rest house of sorts where she spent the night cheerfully, not in the least perturbed by the noises.

She had learned enough to set off again very early in the morning, before the day had really heated. She hoisted her rucksack and stepped out on the road to the south; having done Syria, all that remained was to do Jordan, then Israel, whence she planned to take ship to Istanbul and, after doing Turkey, to work back through Greece to Western Europe.

There was a great deal of traffic on the road south, much of it military. It was clearly pointless to jerk a thumb at a convoy of tank transporters or troop trucks, but she tried it on everything else. For a while, nothing stopped. Then a very old truck, with half a dozen Arabs squatting in the back, pulled up by the roadside for her.

"Anybody speak English?" Shirle asked cheerfully.

There was one who did, to some extent. Shirle climbed aboard and squatted next to him, smiling at him, and he grinning sheepishly. The smell in the truck was pungent, but never mind. This was adventure, well out of the tourist rut, and *fun*. She endeavored to learn the English-speaker's name. It was long, difficult to remember, but in the middle of it was an Al. "I'll call you Al," she told him.

The man looked around the rest of the truckload, then spluttered in Arabic, and they all laughed hugely. Shirle was delighted. They were getting along just fine. It was going to be a success. She started to tell Al, in simple words, all about herself; Al passing on a free translation to his comrades.

At the word "American" they all looked startled. One began a rapid Arabic expostulation. From Al's confused interpretation, Shirle at last gathered that this was an attack on the United States, its policy, Israel, and imperialism. Shirle shook her head vigorously and started on an account of her country's virtues. Al struggled manfully with the translation. The comrades began to listen with more respect. The phenomenon of an unprotected woman traveling by herself yielded to, and indeed reinforced, the even greater wonder of the power, the benevolence, and the goodwill of the American nation. By the time they reached the Jordan frontier, Shirle was convinced that she had persuaded them. She sang them an American song. In response, after some embarrassment, they started on a long singsong of their own. As they mouthed, Shirle gazed at them affectionately. What were they but a bunch of simple, charming peasants? What was their cause but a peasant's longing to recover his lost fields?

Once across the frontier, the truck soon swung off the road onto a track that led to a laager of such vehicles outside a vast array of small huts crammed with people. Suddenly she understood. Refugees.

A dark, scowling Arab came toward them, a machine gun slung over his shoulder. He gestured angrily toward Shirle. Al climbed down from the truck and a long explanation followed, merging into a tirade from the scowler. Shirle got down and joined Al. "Tell him I'm on vacation and you gave me a lift," she suggested.

But that seemed beyond Al's competence. He shrugged and turned to submit once more to his superior's harangue. After a time, Shirle settled down on the rough ground, unhitching her rucksack and using it as a backrest. A small crowd of women and wondering children gathered round her, giggling nervously.

More men had joined the argument. At last Al came across, followed by two villainous-looking Arabs with pistols at their belts. These two, Al explained, were to drive her to the nearest railway station at Mafraq.

Shirle eyed them doubtfully. "I'd rather stay with you," she told Al. "Drive me back to the main road and I'll thumb another lift."

But Al miserably shook his head. These two would take her. He turned away. Shirle had half decided to start walking to the main road, but the two men took her arms and lifted her into a jeep, flinging her rucksack into the back. Making the best of it, she asked brightly if either spoke English. There was no response. So she contented herself with smiling benignly at them and gazing at the scene.

On the main road there was plenty of traffic. But after about a mile the driver swung his jeep onto a side road, deserted. Hey, demanded Shirle, what was this! But the other man merely replied, "Mafraq."

Yet another mile, and the driver suddenly pulled off the road and halted among some rocks. She saw to her alarm that the other man was leering at her. She tried to jump down to run, but the driver caught her, dragged her from the vehicle, pinned her against a rock. The other, still leering, stood in front of her, ripped away her shawl, began to tear open her bodice. She struggled obstinately, refusing to scream; but helpless.

Then she heard the sound of an engine. Around a bend came an armored car, followed by a jeep; men in uniform.

So she screamed. When one of the Arabs shoved his filthy hand across her mouth, she bit it deeply, and screamed.

The armored car's gun swung, there was a splutter of shots. The two Arabs released her, running for their own jeep, firing their pistols wildly, inaccurately, uselessly. From the ground, to which she had dropped for cover, Shirle saw them clamber into their jeep, race it away down the road, the armored car spurting after it.

The other army vehicle came toward her, a young officer jumped out, lifted her up, speaking in Arabic.

Striving not to sob, Shirle asked, "Do you speak English?"

"Yes, of course. You are English?"

"American. I'm on my college vacation."

He smiled gently. He was a handsome young man, though short—quite several inches shorter than she.

"It is unwise for a tourist to go alone, especially here in the north, and especially a woman. You are going to Amman? That is best. Your American embassy is there."

"I won't go to the embassy," she assured him, recovering her calm. "Is there a Y.W. in Amman?"

"A Y.W.?"

"Y.W.C.A. Hostel for girls."

"Ah, yes, I think there is one."

He was interrupted by a burst of fire down the road. He smiled at her. "They will not now trouble anybody."

"Good Lord," she murmured. The thought came to her that this was indeed something to relate to Eleanor when she got back to college. She doubted if even Eleanor could match this.

The young officer said, "I am on a mission to my regimental camp, just south of Amman. I will take you."

He put her in the seat beside the driver and himself climbed into the back of the jeep. The armored car was waiting for them half a mile along the road, starting ahead when they reached it, one of the soldiers holding aloft Shirle's rucksack, which he had recovered from the Palestinians' jeep.

That jeep had swung off the road and overturned, wrecked. Shirle tried not to look just beyond it where two corpses lay twisted on the bleak ground.

§

The young officer, who gave her his name, Sayid al Zouqa, leaned over from the rear, chatting to her, telling her sadly of his country's plight; but soon the army would assert itself and put things right.

They were moving south along a minor road, skirting the mountains. It was a rough road, Sayid agreed, but without much traffic; military convoys were creating great delays on the main road. Also he intended to break his journey for half an hour to call on his uncle, to make sure that he was secure. His uncle had once been a soldier, loyal to his king, and a very brave man. But now he was old, and he lived in a farmhouse a few miles along the road, with not many people around him; and wild bands of fedayin were roaming the mountains.

The valley along which they were traveling had a small stream running and was fertile with olive groves, orchards, and barley. The farmhouse at which they halted was square, white, well-kept. The grave servant who opened the door welcomed the young officer. "Colonel Zouqa is in the garden, with two guests."

They passed through the cool dimness of the house into the dazzle of the small walled garden, where three Arabs were seated at a round table bearing a jug of iced sherbet. One of them, Shirle saw as her eyes adjusted to the glare, was elderly, suave, evidently the uncle. The two others were rough-looking, pistols at their belts, chins unshaven.

Shirle checked in astonishment, staring at one of them.

"Giles!" she exclaimed, but uncertainly.

The man gave no sign of recognition. Shirle stood there, puzzled, while Sayid went forward to speak in Arabic to his uncle. The man she had taken for Giles joined in the talk. Shirle was nonplussed.

In a few minutes Sayid returned to her.

"My uncle bids you welcome and asks you to have food in his house with me. He asks to be excused himself, for he has business with his two other guests."

"Sure," agreed Shirle reluctantly, still looking at the trio.

"Something is wrong?" Sayid asked as he took her into the house, where food was already set on a table.

"It's one of those men talking to your uncle. He's not an Arab. He's English. His name's Giles Dunton."

"You must be mistaken."

"But I can't be. He was on the ship with me from Marseilles to Beirut. I got to know him real well." She looked at Sayid, smiling. "We went to bed together every night."

She thought the young man was shocked. That surprised her. But then he shook his head and assured her again that she was mistaken.

"He is a Palestinian. I can tell you for certain. I heard him speaking with my uncle. By his speaking words, I know he is from Palestine."

"Then all I can say," declared Shirle, "is that it's the most doggone likeness that I ever did see in my whole life."

11

When Kennard's report reached London, Colonel Chase had reluctantly to admit that he could no longer play this one alone. So he crossed the road to see Sandiman at the Foreign and Commonwealth Office, and gave him an outline.

Sandiman asked, "You think it must be Arafat they're after?"

"I'm guessing. I could be wrong."

"Could you be wrong over the whole thing?"

Chase shrugged. "Possibly. Are you suggesting we should risk it?"

After a pause, Sandiman admitted, "No. One sees that's impossible. The only question is, how widely do we disclose? If in the end it comes to nothing . . ."

"Let's hope so."

"Of course, but what then do we say?"

Chase looked around for a windowsill to sit on, and clasped his hands between his knees. "The facts are scarcely arguable. Those two men have gone to the Lebanon, and probably by now beyond, intent on violence. There can be little doubt that they intend to kill a leading Arab."

"We tell the Americans first, I suppose," said Sandiman, sighing. "After all, it's their peace plan. Some people wouldn't mind too much if that were scuppered. Except for the violence, naturally."

Chase said nothing. He well knew that Sandiman was one of the Foreign Office Arabists—for good, hardheaded reasons, chiefly for oil.

Sandiman added, "Even if they're found, can they be stopped? After all, they've done nothing—yet."

"You can leave that to us," Chase mildly assured him. "The trouble is finding them."

"The Jordanians next, or simultaneously," Sandiman mused. "That little man in Hussein's palace. How about the Egyptians? You don't really suppose, do you, that Nasser could be the target? The heavens would open if he were done. How about our lords and masters?"

"I'm reporting to the Prime Minister at Chequers tonight. My recommendation will be to play it in as low a key as possible. I hope it can be kept on my sort of level, not the diplomatic."

"Probably better."

"The Egyptians will be all right," Chase said, "provided we can pass the information quietly to the policeman I have in mind. I'm not so sure of the Jordanians. I know whom you mean in the palace. Absolutely sound, do you think?"

"Yes," Sandiman replied. "Although I'm not sure it mightn't be better to slip the word to the King direct."

"I'm really rather strongly against bringing it to diplomatic level."

"That can be avoided," said Sandiman, "if we get the necessary authority."

"The Prime Minister? I think he'll be convinced. It would help if your master took our line with him."

"I'll put the case to him," Sandiman promised. "The difficulty, of course, is the Palestinians themselves . . ."

"You mean, you might as well broadcast it on the BBC World Service," Chase agreed, "and send a full text to the Kremlin, and possibly a copy to Peking."

Sandiman regarded him gravely. "What you're saying, Colonel, is that we should refrain from warning the one man we think most likely to be the target."

"Looked at sensibly, yes. What more can Arafat do to protect himself from attempts on his life? He expects them all the time and lives in a posse of gunmen. His best chance lies in our quietly finding the Duntons and, shall we say, dissuading them. If the Russians are let in, I doubt if we can."

"Point taken," Sandiman agreed. "Success for the Duntons would work quite well for them. Arafat isn't really their man. All right, I'll make your case to my master."

"Thanks, " said Chase, rising. "I started by thinking this was a mere nonsense. Now I want to get all the pressure put on that I can."

§

Harvey Kennard realized, when he got his orders, that the heat was now being turned up. He smiled. At least it was now being acknowledged by the top brass that he had been right in the first place.

"We're to go to Amman," he told Miller. "They've arranged to get us over the frontiers without questions. We're to steer clear of the embassy. They've booked us a room at the Intercontinental Hotel."

Miller approved. "Much more comfortable. It's a super hotel."

"My message says you'll know the man in Amman to consult."

"He's a fellow named Chapman," Miller told him. "Officially he's working for the British Council, all very cultural."

"He'll put us onto the right man in King Hussein's service. And we're also to work in with an American who'll get in touch, identity not yet known."

"Right," said Miller. "Start at first light tomorrow? I'll pick you up."

Once they had left Damascus behind and headed south over the desert, Kennard was grateful for the car's air conditioning. The midday heat was nearly unbearable.

The road traffic was mostly jeeps or trucks laden with well-armed guerrillas, and a few staff cars resplendent with officers. At Kiswe, where the road ran briefly alongside the Hejaz railway, long columns of infantry were standing in line to board the wagons of a waiting train. Ten miles farther on Miller had to maneuver for nearly half an hour past a military convoy traveling south—Russian tanks on the transporters, rocket launchers, light artillery. Troops were squatting on the truck floors, crowded together, staring impassively, bristling like hedgehogs with rifles, automatics, the squat ugliness of mortars.

"Syrian army," said Miller. "They're massing on the Jordan border—three brigades, it's thought, one of them armored. If it comes to a showdown, Arafat can almost certainly count on an invasion from Syria."

"You think there will be a showdown?"

"Difficult to say. Jordan has been on the verge of it for months, but it never seems to happen. In Beirut, our people think it could drag on like that indefinitely, unless there's some really outstanding dramatic event, some catalyst to start the thing off."

"Such as?"

"God knows."

The Syrian guards at the frontier made no trouble, and when they were identified at the Jordan post, an officer spoke briefly to Miller in Arabic.

"He was warning us," Miller told Kennard when they were moving again, "to get past the northern towns as fast as we can. There's already trouble between the guerrillas and Hussein's armored brigade camped nearby. If that escalates, there'll be a bloody massacre. They're all round the refugee camps, which are always guerrilla headquarters—crammed full of women and children."

As they drove south toward Amman, through hordes of Arafat's men in their dirty olive-green jackets, machine guns slung from their shoulders, Kennard noted with ironic interest men and women working patiently in the fields, ignoring the shifting military scene. There must have been men and women toiling like that in those fields, he reflected, while battles raged around them, ever since the hunting nomads of prehistory first began tilling the stony soil. Here was where it had all started.

And here, he added wryly to himself as they reached Amman, was what it had all led up to. Along the narrow, twisting streets of old Arab houses had been built modern apartment blocks in the glass-and-concrete manner. Slender minarets probed into the skyline; in the valleys and on the slopes below them rose the square, glazed towers of modernity.

"Amman's like Rome," explained Miller, "built on seven hills. Each district is a hill—Jebel this or Jebel that. The business and shopping area is mostly in the central valley, down there. Two vast Palestinian refugee camps stand on the hills of the northern outskirts, at Jebel Wahdat and Jebel Hussein. The fashionable district is Jebel Amman. We're coming to it now. That's where the hotel is."

Already they were in streets of expensive-looking villas and new apartment blocks. The Intercontinental Hotel itself outdid them all—balconies and beautifully curtained windows, flowers blooming in concrete pots, white-painted garden furniture on the terraces, and the deep blue of the pool.

The foyer was crowded, noisy. Miller recognized several newsmen. "They must be expecting it to explode."

When they were in their room he suggested to Kennard, "You ought to call it a day. You look done in."

But Kennard wearily shook his head. "Give me an hour to take a shower and change my clothes. Then bring the man we have to meet."

"If you say so. Chapman's on tap. But I still think you ought to rest."

"In one hour," said Kennard, going to the phone. He called room service. "Send up a bottle of scotch, soda water, and ice."

§

An American came with Roy Chapman. He was introduced as Ned Bartholomew; tall, thin, smiling, amiable, very handsome, intelligent-looking, Harvard-graduate type, and probably quite unscrupulous. Chapman was long-haired, plump, carefully groomed in gabardines, probably a queer, and supercilious, almost condescending.

Reluctantly, Kennard started on the story, but Chapman interrupted. "We know the background. We've been briefed."

"Good. That saves me trouble."

Kennard wondered whether his brusqueness was simply the product of a long journey, the exhausting heat.

The American smoothed it. "It's damned important to stop them. We're extremely grateful to you British for latching onto it. The Secretary of State himself has been told, and will inform the President. I'm sure a private word of thanks will go from the White House to Downing Street. On our lowly level, the same goes from me to you."

"The job's still to be done," said Kennard. "How do we stand now? Put me in the picture. I've spent the day traveling. Bloody awful country, isn't it?"

"A gauche judgment," protested Chapman. "Charming people—I speak of the Bedouin, of course. Magnificently harsh scenery. Archeologically unsurpassed."

"Maybe. But it's not ancient ruins we're digging for." Pointedly Kennard turned to the American. "I take it the Jordan authorities have been informed. Anybody else?"

"I think your people have slipped a word to the Egyptians. We're not persona overgrata in that quarter these days."

"The Palestinians?"

"No. It's vital to keep the Russians out of it."

Kennard nodded. He asked Chapman, "Do we know where Arafat is?"

"Only that he's almost certainly here in Amman. After the attempt on the King's life last Tuesday, the army broke out a bit. Some of their light armored units came blazing into the city and knocked hell out of the El Fatah buildings. It was a joy to watch. Arafat and several of his top boys were in a

133 •

building near the marketplace. It was shelled to buggery, but they all got away. Now Arafat has gone underground."

"But still in Amman? Then the Duntons will be moving here, if they're not here already. They've good sources of information, that's for sure. The Jordan authorities probably know who. Whom do I see?"

"His name's Badir," Chapman told him. "He holds no actual post on the King's staff, but looks after a lot of the backstairs work, and he's a real power in the land. I've made a provisional date for twelve noon tomorrow, at the Basman Palace—that's the King's business headquarters."

Bartholomew asked, "Do you feel sure it's Arafat they're aiming to kill?"

"On the basis of what we know, he seems likeliest."

"It would set back any hope of peace for a generation," said the American. "He's the only leader of quality the Palestinians have. If he went, the Marxists and Maoists would take over."

"You know Arafat?" asked Kennard.

"I've met him. Nobody really knows him. He's a remarkable man in his way—educated, fluent in four or five languages, sufficient of a politician to keep control of a million or so Palestinian refugees and the half dozen private armies. He has, too, the one quality that Arabs respect above all others—personal austerity."

"How?"

"He lives without possessions, other than the clothes he wears and his guns. They say he rarely sleeps more than a couple of hours a night. He eats little. I just don't know how he got that belly."

"A good soldier?"

"Nobody really knows. He hasn't ever fought a battle. He was in some minor skirmishes against you British at the time of Suez. Apart from that, his sort of fighting is a raiding party by night over the Israel frontier to blow up a bridge or attack an isolated police post. He had very little to do with the set-piece wars against Israel. Of course, his testing time may be coming now quite soon."

"He'll need to be a bloody good soldier," put in Chapman, "when he comes up against Hussein's Bedouin."

Kennard reached for the whiskey. "Anybody like another drink?"

§

Miller drove him to the Basman Palace at noon next day, but Kennard went alone to his interview with the man named Badir; an elderly man, plump, cautiously noncommittal. Kennard responded with equal caution. Within minutes he felt sure that, even if Badir did not know exactly where the Duntons were, he knew the men to whom they had probably gone—and intended to do nothing about it.

"We are on the edge of the abyss of civil war, Mr. Kennard. All our energies are absorbed in striving to avert it. We wish you success in your objective, but I know you will understand the precariousness, the fragility of the present moment in our country."

Kennard regarded him in silence. It was understandable, of course. What, after all, could suit the Jordan authorities better, if the Palestinians started a revolt, than the assassination of their leader? The guerrillas would probably crumble away in confusion and chaos, and the army could take the opportunity to clear them out of Jordan's towns and villages, back into the refugee camps.

The telephone rang on Badir's desk. He spoke quickly

into it, listened, raised his eyebrows in gentle astonishment, then apologized to Kennard. "There is something which needs my attention without delay. I shall hope for another meeting before you leave Amman."

Kennard hesitated for a moment, then chanced an exaggeration. "Mr. Badir, this operation is being directed, on our side, by our Prime Minister personally. If it should fail, and I were forced to report that the Jordan authorities withheld full cooperation, you can imagine how unfortunate that would be for relations between our two countries." He saw that the little fat man was uncertain. "I don't for a moment suppose that you know the whereabouts of the two men I am looking for, Mr. Badir. But should I be far out in suggesting that you do know the undercover organization which is probably aiding them? Put me in touch."

"I could make some guesses, perhaps. But you must excuse me. There is a crisis which needs my immediate attention."

"Give me a name, Mr. Badir."

He hesitated. Then, "Very well. Colonel Moustafa Nabavi."

"Where?"

"He is attached to the 40th Armored Brigade, now stationed in the camp to the south of Irbid."

"Thank you. May I have some authority from you, so that Colonel Nabavi will cooperate?"

Badir scribbled a note in Arabic on a paper bearing the palace emblem. "Now go, please. I must hasten to His Majesty."

"What's the crisis?"

Badir hesitated again, then threw up his hands. "Why not? What can it matter now? In a few hours my country will be in flames. The Palestinians have hijacked an American airliner over Belgium, with 150 people on board. It was bound for New York."

Kennard was puzzled at the urgency. "It's not the first skyjacking."

"They are bringing it here, Mr. Kennard. And before the day is out there will be three more international airliners hijacked and flown here. These madmen will hold hundreds of Americans hostage in the Jordan desert. I know, I tell you. I have sources among the Palestinians, naturally. Please go now."

When he got back into the car Kennard told Miller briefly. Miller gawped.

"You spoke of a catalyst that could start civil war. Will this do?"

"It's a cinch."

"Then we make for Irbid, fastest," said Kennard. "I have to get to a certain Colonel Moustafa Nabavi before he becomes otherwise engaged."

12

The old man, Zouqa, had been startled when the American girl recognized Giles in the garden, no doubt of that. So had Mark.

"Just bad luck," Giles told them. "She was a passenger in the ship I took from Marseilles. A college girl on vacation, trying to see the country through the eyes of its people."

Zouqa was too polite to say any more. But Mark growled. Just before they went to sleep that night, in a room in Colonel Zouqa's farmhouse, he took Giles up on it. "I suppose you were banging that girl's arse all the way to Beirut."

"What you should suppose," replied Giles irritably, "is to mind your own business."

Again Mark growled. To have added to the risk for such a reason! More and more, as the days passed, he found himself thinking of Helen, and regretting the sense of family loyalty which had involved him. "For God's sake, Giles, couldn't you have done without a woman for just a few days? We're taking enough chances without that."

"There's no extra risk."

"There is. She recognized you."

"She thought for a moment that she had. When I went on talking Arabic to the old man, she decided she was mistaken. I was watching her eyes. Forget it, and go to sleep."

But Mark lay long awake. Anthony was dead, finished. The idea of revenge was absurd, merely primitive, accomplishing nothing. Giles had this grandiose idea that it could help stem the grotesque terrorism of the Palestinians. Even if it could, what was that to him? He was too deeply in, of course, to contemplate getting out now. The only possibility was to see the thing through, and then get back into his own clothes in the hired car in the garage at Zahle, and into his own life. He mused sadly to himself, thought of Helen, turned on his side, and at last slept.

It was scarcely dawn when one of Zouqa's servants woke them. Giles rolled from his bed, yawning, remarking that at least they didn't have to waste time cleaning themselves, or shaving. In another day or two they would have acquired the correct smell.

Zouqa awaited them in a room where a table was laid with coffee, a dish of dates, pots of honey, and cakes of flat Arab bread. While they ate, he unfolded a map on the table. "The main highway south is to be avoided. It is jammed with military convoys and Palestinians. You must cross it here, close to Jerash, then travel east into the Black Desert. There are no roads, but only tracks, see here on this map."

Giles said, "I knew something of the desert, long ago, and I doubt if it has changed much. Marshland in winter, crusting into salt pans as it dries out. Mudflats. Black basalt outcropping everywhere. In summer, inches of choking dust over the hard ground."

Zouqa nodded. "The desert does not change. You see this

track here, and the branch here to the right? It leads close to Qasr Hallabat."

"One of a string of hunting lodges," Giles explained to Mark, "built by the caliphs a thousand years ago."

"More than a thousand," said Zouqa.

"In ruins now, of course. But the structures still standing. Wonderful refuges. Our destination is Hallabat, Colonel? I think I can find my way there. Isn't that where the R.A.F. made an airstrip, soon after the end of the war?"

"The airstrip is farther north, and east of Hallabat, but in that direction."

"I was put down twice by the R.A.F. on that airstrip, long ago, and made my way through the desert. And when we reach Hallabat?"

"A Colonel Nabavi, who is stationed at the military post at Qasr el Azraq, will come to Hallabat to supply you with what you asked for."

"Today?"

"I hope so. If not, wait until tomorrow. If he does not come tomorrow, we cannot help you further." The old man sighed. "In the chaos that threatens our country, who can tell what is possible today and may become impossible tomorrow?"

Giles nodded. "Understood. Are you sure that Yassir Arafat is in Amman?"

"Not sure. He is forever moving. But my information is that he has found a new, secret headquarters, somewhere in the poorer part of Amman, in the valley that lies between Jebel Amman and Jebel Webdeh."

"Can you give us a contact in Amman?"

"Not as things are now. All I can give you is a refuge, if you need one. I have my house for the town in a quiet street on the slopes of Jebel Webdeh. I have written here the directions. It is not a modern house. My father built it when the old emir decided to make his capital city from a village and a camel market. There is a stable, and above it a small loft, with a hidden entrance. There you will be in good refuge."

"Is the house locked?"

"I have there a servant named Qasim. He will know of you and admit you. If you pay him, he will supply you with food. There is no more that I can do."

"It is more than I could hope," replied Giles. "My brother and I are greatly in your debt."

§

Early in the day as it was, the road around Jerash was noisy with slow-moving convoys and a multitude of tattered vehicles. All Mark could get was an impression of the pillars, broken columns, arches and steps of the Roman avenue and forum, marvelously pale against the brown hillside dotted with dark trees and white houses.

Soon after, to his relief, Giles directed him onto a side road, almost empty; then they were out on the tracks of the desert. By now the heat was engulfing, but there was no noise save that of their own vehicle, and an occasional distant whisper of heavy artillery.

After a rough ride of perhaps ten miles along desert tracks, Giles pointed forward. "Hallabat."

The ruined walls, dun-colored, pierced here and there with the blackness of window embrasures, topped a small hillock, around the base of which clustered a few stunted trees.

Giles put his hand on his brother's arm. "Hold it."

Two vehicles stood by the ruins, an armored car and a utility.

"Nabavi?" asked Mark uneasily.

"We'll have to risk it. Drive up close to the utility. There are men in it. I'll put the question in Arabic. If it's Nabavi, I'll switch to English. If there's any doubt, I'll give the word to go, and race like the devil for that clump of bushes on the right. Then we can get cover from the slope of the hill. I don't think they'd bother to follow us. All we'd get is a few chaser shots."

Mark engaged the lowest gear and edged the jeep across rough ground to the ruin. In the utility were two officers and a driver. Giles leaned out and spoke rapidly; then turned to Mark. "It's our man. He wants our jeep behind the shelter of that wall."

Giles got out to greet Nabavi. The utility driver, helped by two men from the armored car, unloaded three canvas sacks and brought them behind the wall to the jeep. Giles came around with Nabavi. He read the list the other had given him, and Mark checked from the sacks as the men opened them.

"Two Kaleshnikov machine guns with ample ammunition. A dozen hand grenades—British army grenades, I see. A dozen hand-propelled smoke canisters. Two automatic pistols . . ."

"They're Browning nine millimeter," said Mark.

"Useful enough if we get close. A magazine loaded into each, and fifteen spare magazines, each of eight rounds."

"Check," said Mark.

Giles turned to thank Nabavi. The colonel replied with a few curt sentences. When he had returned to his own car, and the two army vehicles were driven off, Mark asked Giles, "What did he say at the end? I could get only the bit about praying that we would prosper in our endeavors."

Giles grinned. "It was an ancient Arab request. He asked us, if we get the bastard, to twist off his balls and stuff them in his mouth before we shoot him. Let's get this ammunition stowed into the jeep. We can carry the guns. The sooner now we get off to Amman, the better."

Before they started, Giles walked to the end of the wall and looked out.

"Hold it," he said. "Best switch off."

Mark joined him. Giles's cautious arm stayed him in the shelter of the wall. Moving toward them from the south, perhaps a mile away, were a couple of trucks, followed by a dust plume that signified several more.

"If we got cracking the way we came," said Mark, "and took it fast, we could be on the main road in half an hour."

For answer, Giles dropped to the ground and edged around the wall, then wriggled back.

"No good. There's another lot coming in from the west."

"We could run for it to the north, then circle back."

"Too risky. We don't know what there is ahead. There must be something on. With luck, they'll pass without troubling us."

"If we could get the jeep further into cover . . ."

But it was too late. One of the trucks had turned and was driving toward them.

"Have to face it out," said Giles. "Squat alongside me by the wall. Leave the talking to me. Drop in an Arabic phrase now and then, but slur it, and say as little as you can."

The truck halted in front of them, the dust cloud drifting everywhere. It was crammed with El Fatah men, all with machine guns or rifles, all jubilant. There were three on the driving seat, as well as the driver.

One of them leaned out and flowed Arabic at Giles, who responded gravely. Mark could not get much of what the guerrilla was saying, but he picked up most of Giles's answers. They were brothers, refugees from Palestine, their homeland Gaza. They were going south to Amman, under orders from the leader; Giles used Arafat's revolutionary name, Abu Ammar.

But his replies did not seem to satisfy the guerrillas. A rapid argument was developing. Of the three passengers in the driving cab, the one in the middle was persistent; a thin, very dark, mean-faced fellow with suspicious eyes. Giles kept his answers calm, but the other voices were rising angrily. A guerrilla in the back of the truck swung his machine gun forward. Then Giles rose slowly and gestured Mark to get into the jeep. The truck turned slowly and moved north.

"Follow," muttered Giles. "Explain later."

When they were moving, and he could safely speak English, he told Mark, "There's a big force of them gathering for some special show. I couldn't get them to say what. Then one of them, the evil-looking sod in the front, started to raise suspicions. Without him, we'd have got away with it."

"Did he suspect that we're fake?"

"No. They don't doubt that we're Palestinians. What they obviously think is that we're some sort of spies—for Hussein, or for the army. So they won't leave us behind. Wherever it is they're heading, and whatever's going to happen, we have to be there, within sight."

"Could we turn suddenly and make a dash for it?"

"Not on, I'm afraid. The bastards in that truck have at least a dozen machine guns. At a range of fifty yards, however wild the shooting, the risk'd be too great. Anyway, we'd be turning into the next lot coming up behind. We'll have to string along and wait for an opportunity."

§

About an hour later the truck halted. Mark pulled up as far short of it as he dared. Other trucks were stopping around them. Yet more were wheeling and forming a separate laager about four hundred yards ahead. Men were climbing down from all the trucks, kindling oil fires in buckets of sand, swinging out cooking pots, jabbering, shouting.

Mark got food and drink from the jeep. As the day darkened the hubbub seemed to grow around the winking flares from the oil fires. From the distant laager came a few ragged shots, then faint shouting; but it all died away.

One bunch moved toward the brothers, the leader swinging a storm lantern. It was the suspicious one who had first accosted them.

Giles received them with ceremony, inviting them to sit in a semicircle before him, regretting he had no coffee to offer them. Mark went to the jeep, making a pretense of busying himself with the stores. He could not, therefore, hear everything that was said, and could make out only part of what he could hear. The talk seemed to be about Gaza, some of the men questioning Giles, and he answering with seeming readiness. Then Giles twisted the talk, taking over the questions. This Mark grasped. He was trying to discover the purpose of the gathering of so many in this remote part of the desert. One man began to answer volubly and happily, something about aircraft. But at once the suspicious one silenced him. Not long afterward they rose and made off.

Giles came back, whistling softly. "We're in a spot. I think they're almost sure now that we're army spies. Our friend brought over a couple of men from Gaza, questioning me about the place. I did fairly well. I once knew it intimately—but so long ago. I must have made several gaffes. So I tried to turn the talk to what this is all about. It's something to do with hijacked aircraft, though God knows what."

"We make a break for it?"

"Not tonight. We'd never make it in the dark. The danger is they'll come for us. We'd better stand watches. You keep from now until midnight. Wake me then, and I'll keep until six. Once we can see what's happening, we can decide how to make a break. We're going to have to, that's sure."

He got two blankets from the jeep, threw one to Mark, wrapped himself in the other, and stretched out on the ground, muttering that it was going to be damned cold.

Mark twisted the blanket round his shoulders and sat watching the darkness, pitted with flickers of flame and alive with moving shadows. He hung a couple of grenades at his belt and nursed his machine gun across his knees. Gradually the hubbub lessened. The new moon, risen briefly, had set. But the clear desert sky was gleaming with stars, so that although the little flames on the ground were gradually dying out, he could still see moving figures.

But none approached. There was no attack. At midnight he roused Giles with a whisper that there had been no trouble. Then he rolled the blanket around him, stretched out, and went to sleep.

He woke with the light. Giles was a few yards away, talking to some men in a nearby truck, bartering for some coffee as one of them relit the sand bucket and brewed up.

Giles returned with two tin mugs of it, hot and strong. As they sipped, he told Mark, "Now I've got it. I began to tumble to it during the night. The flat stretch between us and the bunch over in the distance is the old R.A.F. airstrip. Dawson's Field, it was called. The A.O.C.-in-C. at that time was named Dawson. These fellows are calling it El

Thawra—Revolution Airport. There are to be hijackings. The men I spoke to knew that, but nothing more. Hijacked aircraft—from Europe probably—are to be brought here to be held hostage. That much is clear."

"And these are the guards to hold off any rescue attempt by the army?"

"I take it so. You see what it means for us?"

"We must get out before the army puts a ring round the lot. Now, do you reckon?"

"Not yet," Giles replied. "They're too strong behind us. But I gathered from my chums with the coffee that there's to be a great meeting later. They're waiting for something. These fellows don't know what. Then they're all going to gather. That'll be the moment."

It came shortly after noon. There was a shout from a truck by the edge of the airstrip. Mark noticed that it had now sprouted radio antennae. From all around, men were surging toward the truck. A tall guerrilla climbed onto its roof and harangued.

"Now?" asked Mark.

Giles frowned. Three trucks, still manned, were stationed behind them, standing guard. The ill-favored, suspicious guerrilla stood by the central vehicle.

Mark eased a grenade from his belt.

"I'll go over to ask them something. When I'm about ten yards from them, come in the jeep, fast." He saw that Giles was hesitating, reluctant to put him to the risk. "Don't be an ass, Giles. I was doing this only a couple of years ago, not a couple of decades. Ready? I'm going now."

He walked slowly across the intervening ground, smiling at the guerrillas. One or two gun muzzles swung hesitantly, but he shouted reassurance in a few Arabic phrases he knew.

147 •

The moment he heard the jeep's motor whirr he flung the grenade, dropped to the ground for the explosion, then opened up with his machine gun.

Most of them lay twisted on the ground or slumped over the rails of the trucks. Three were running in terror.

Mark jumped up and turned toward the jeep. As he did so, one of the three fugitives twisted around in desperation, firing wildly. Mark felt the sting in his thigh, stumbled, and fell.

A machine gun crackled behind him and the guerrilla somersaulted over. That was from Giles, now beside him, hoisting him swiftly into the car, jumping in, and racing south.

From where he lay in the back of the jeep, Mark could see firing from the crowd round the radio van. But the distance was too great for accuracy. A couple of trucks started in pursuit, but neither was fast enough. He saw Giles's face, grim and set, as he drove. He was scanning the desert closely, as though looking for a landmark.

"Hang on," he said. "I know where we can hide. It's not far, and I'm sure I'm on the way. Are you all right?"

"Yes, okay," said Mark. Then the pain became intense and he passed out.

13

The road north from Amman, Kennard thought, was less congested than when they came south the day before. Army convoys were moving slowly in either direction, but the dust-stained trucks full of guerrillas seemed mostly to be heading north. Some twenty-five miles from Amman, indeed, many of the Palestinian trucks turned off the road and took desert tracks eastward. There was a holdup while a squadron of armored cars and other army vehicles also crossed the road and headed into the desert.

"Whatever it is, it's over there," said Miller.

"It can only be the skyjacks. At least it's clearing the road a bit for us. Another dozen miles, then we turn off west to find the 40th Armored—somewhere south of Irbid, near the Syrian frontier, Badir said. It shouldn't be too difficult to find an armored brigade."

Nor was it, when Kennard realized the strength of Badir's signature on that crested paper. At the second military laager they tried, the commanding officer hastened over to their car. "Colonel Nabavi? He's not 40th Armored, sir."

149 •

"Attached."

"Ah. Then I'll give you an escort to the brigadier. He'll know."

He shouted an order and a scout car swiveled in front of them.

Kennard had been aware for some time of distant artillery fire. Now it was a crescendo. Soon they were threading through an extended line of heavy gun positions, firing over the ridge of a hill. On the other side they came to the action. A few tanks were dug in, but most were maneuvering cautiously. The return fire was sharp, most of it rockets. A couple of tanks were burning, two smudges of oily black smoke. At that moment, over to the right, another was struck by a rocket. It erupted into flames, the crew tumbling out, running for cover.

The rockets seemed to be firing from the outskirts of a huge refugee camp, to the rear of which crowds were hastening back toward the town on the horizon, presumably Irbid, as army shells smashed into the vast compound of small huts. Kennard could not see, from that distance, whether the fleeing refugees were mostly women, but he assumed they were, since packs of children were running desperately with them.

The scout car led toward a hummock from the shelter of which several officers were studying the terrain through field glasses. An adjutant came to stop them, but, when the driver of the scout car had spoken, hurried back to the group. A senior officer walked over. "I cannot help you. Colonel Nabavi is not here."

"But Mr. Badir said—"

"Nabavi was here this morning. But you have heard of the hijacked airliners?"

"Only briefly," said Kennard.

"It is most grave. One aircraft has already landed in the desert and there are rumors that another is coming. We are getting a little news by radio, and our instructions. I have sent Nabavi with all the armor I can spare. As you see, we are engaged here—and getting too much fire."

"It is is urgent that I find him."

The officer hesitated. Kennard handed him Badir's authority.

"There is a landing strip in the desert which your Air Force made many years ago, and which has long been unused," he said, handing the paper back. "It is there. I will tell your escort."

The officer spoke to the driver of the scout car, who saluted and started his engine.

"Thanks," said Kennard."

§

The ride across the desert was rough. They were in the wrong vehicle for that work. Several times Miller, swearing to himself, only just managed to keep the car from sliding into one of the numerous deep ruts with which the parched ground was streaked, or slipping down the slope of a wadi. Although it was late afternoon, the heat was still fierce and frequently they were stifled in thick dust-fog from convoys heading in the same direction.

Because of the going, the journey took more than two hours. Kennard was wondering whether they would make it before nightfall when, emerging from an eddy of dust, he saw a line of armored cars drawn up in a wide arc about a mile ahead; he could dimly make out beyond them the wide wingspread of a grounded aircraft.

A few minutes later came the drone of engines in the distance, then another aircraft was circling, descending, as though hesitant. Miller whistled incredulously.

"He'll never get her down in the middle of that lot."

But he did. The liner came in low, touched, bounced, then with flaps hard down and engines grimly gunning, sped across the rough runway and at last pulled up, turned, taxied close to the liner already grounded, so that two pairs of wings topped the frenzied, excited throngs; the shouting and screaming rose as the aircraft's engines cut.

"That's a DC-8," said Miller. "I think the other's a Boeing. Must be panic stations all over the world. This could start anything."

Kennard remained silent. If there should also be a political assassination . . . He was desperately assessing the chances of finding the Duntons through all the turmoil. He thought them slim.

As they followed the scout car, Kennard realized they were traveling round the perimeter of a wide circle of army vehicles and troops, facing inward toward the center, where the stranded aircraft loomed through curtains of dust. But now he could see that, closer in, there was another circle, concentric but facing outward, swarming with guerrillas around dug-in positions. There was no firing either way.

The scout car stopped twice for directions, and at last halted by a couple of armored cars. From one of them an officer walked across to the Englishmen. Nabavi? He nodded, suspicious; but, once he saw Badir's authority, sulkily cooperative. Yes, he had seen the two men. Yes, in Arab dress, like guerrillas. That was yesterday, at Hallabat, a ruined hunting lodge in the desert. He did not know if they were still there or, if not, where they had gone. Their escort could take them there, but not tonight. Impossible, in the conditions they could see for themselves. For tonight they must remain here. He would send a man with blankets.

Miller asked, "Whose are the hijacked aircraft?"

"One is American, one from Switzerland. They say there are to be others."

Miller whistled. "It could start a war."

Nabavi regarded him gravely. "In this country, it must. We have too much tolerated. Now they will let the army fight."

"Starting here?"

He shook his head. "There are three hundred people in the airplanes, which the guerrillas have mined and wired with explosive. If we attack, they say they will blow them up with all the passengers."

"And you believe them?"

"I believe them. Now I will send you blankets and food."

By the time they had eaten it was night. They got back in the car, wrapped themselves in the blankets, talked for a while, but then fell silent, oppressed by the enormity of it all.

On the car radio Miller got the BBC World Service news bulletin. They listened with growing foreboding. The two aircraft in front of them were a TWA Boeing and a Swissair DC-8, both hijacked over Europe on their way to New York. A third hijacked aircraft, a Pan Am jumbo jet, had been put down at Beirut, and the Lebanese were helpless to rescue the 176 people on board, since the guerrillas who had seized it soon after it took off from Amsterdam for New York threatened to blow it up if any attempt were made. There had been a fourth hijack attempt on an El Al Boeing as it crossed the English coast on its way to New York. But it seemed—though reports were confused—that a man had been killed, a woman seized and bound, and the aircraft landed safely at Heathrow. The Palestinians had already announced, in Amman and Beirut, that they were responsible, and that the hijacks were intended to stop the Middle East peace talks.

Kennard switched off the radio. Nagging at him was the increasing fear of the consequences if Arafat were assassinated, in the middle of all this, and the assassins were identified as English. Would the El Fatah madmen, in a frenzy of revenge, blow up these aircraft and massacre the hostages? It seemed far from improbable.

§

There was nobody in the ancient ruin of Hallabat when they drove up to it next morning. Kennard told the driver of the scout car to lead them back to the Amman road, then return to his unit.

The road was already jammed with slow-moving convoys. It took Miller more than three hours to wriggle through. But in the city itself the streets were empty. There was a rumble of shellfire, an occasional ripple of small arms, and on one of the distant hills the flash of rockets.

Miller phoned Roy Chapman to come around to the Intercontinental. He impressed Kennard more favorably than he had before; more sensible, less affected, now that there was action.

"Give us the background."

"A real flap. The Pan Am jumbo hijacked to Beirut was too big to get down in the desert, so they took it to Cairo this morning and blew it up just as the passengers got out down the chutes. Nobody killed, but several women taken to hospital. The Egyptians have arrested the hijackers, three

Palestinians." He laughed shortly. "Nobody supposes anything much will happen to them."

"And at Heathrow?"

"The Israeli plane. The male hijacker was shot dead by an Israeli security man. The woman flung a grenade, but it didn't go off—a dud. They got her out and she's in the jug in London. She's been identified—Leila Khaled."

"The woman who hijacked an American plane to Syria last year?" asked Miller.

"Correct. Not that she has to worry, with three hundred hostages out in the desert. Still, the guerrillas have agreed to release most of the women and children today, about a hundred of them. They're coming to this hotel until they can be flown out." He smiled. "And since practically every major newspaper in the world has sent correspondents, and they'll mostly live here, you're going to have a full dining room."

There was a burst of gunfire close by, a woman screaming, an explosion. Kennard went over to the window. An armored car was moving slowly, firing into a block of flats, from the upper windows of which came return fire.

"What's the situation in the town?" he asked Chapman standing beside him.

"Dicey. Sporadic fighting between guerrillas and troops. This morning the broadcasting building was hit by rockets, but it's back on the air. A few armored cars, like that one, are chasing the guerrillas out from the better quarters of the town, but most of the army is still outside. If they move in, it'll be civil war."

"Arafat?"

"Still in the city somewhere. Informed sources, as they say, think he has a secret hideout near the center, probably on the hill on the other side of this valley, the Jebel Webdeh.

There's an underground radio broadcasting from some-where in that region, and the whole area is strongly held by guerrillas."

"Could the Duntons get to him there?" asked Kennard.

Chapman shrugged. "I'd have said impossible. But they seem to have come through several layers of the impossible already. God knows. But if they did get in, they wouldn't have a cat's chance of getting out again."

A convoy of buses was turning into the front approach to the hotel.

"The women and children from the aircraft," said Chapman.

Kennard nodded, his gaze on the women and children as they moved from the buses into the hotel. They looked weary, heat-stained, creased with anxiety for their men still held in the desert.

"It must have been hell," said Chapman. "The day temperature is well over a hundred, and at night it's bitterly cold. No food, not much to drink, and only aircraft lavatories for three hundred people. Officially, I'm your man. But privately, I hope you don't get to the Duntons before they get to Arafat. It's time somebody paid."

14

When she landed at Bahrain, Helen Dunton almost physically recoiled at the heat. The temperature she had known about, but not the humidity. Within a few steps her shirt was soaked in sweat, clinging to her skin.

The airport building was a relief, and so was the small, modern, efficiently air-conditioned Moustafa Hotel on the holiday coast in the southwest of the island. But by the time she got there she was too limp to do anything but rest and have a meal sent up to her room.

Next morning she took a taxi to the offices of Spooner and Grant, whom Mr. Saunders had named as the bank's corresponding agents. They were in a big block near the port; beyond, an atmosphere of derricks and shipping, cargo unloading and loading; further out in the Gulf a long gray tanker maneuvering.

There was neither a Spooner nor a Grant, but a young English manager named Walters, who managed to suppress his astonishment.

"Mrs. Dunton? Mrs. Mark Dunton? Well, how delightful. I had no idea. . . ."

"There's been a slip-up in communication," she lied to him. "It sounds silly, but Mark and I have missed each other. He wrote on Moustafa Hotel notepaper, so I assumed he was there, but he isn't. So he hasn't had my cable, and he doesn't know I'm here, and I don't know where he's staying."

Walters looked troubled. "You mean, Captain Dunton is in Bahrain?"

"He came more than a week ago. I had a holiday due, so I thought I'd join him." She smiled bravely. "Oh dear, what a muddle!"

"I'm astonished he should have come to Bahrain without contacting me."

"I think it's very confidential business," she said. "Investing oil money. Mr. Saunders said he'd be in touch with you when he had arranged something."

"Oh, good," Walters replied. Privately he was wondering what the hell this was all about. Odd, to say the least. Could it be some obscure method the bank had chosen to check on him? But he dismissed that idea as absurd. Then what on earth . . . ? And the woman seemed strangely nervous, only striving to keep serene.

"He may not be staying in a hotel," she offered. "Mr. Saunders said he might stop with one of his contacts."

"Don't worry," he soothed. "In a community this size . . . I'll have located him by this evening, then you must both dine with my wife and me."

"The business is said to be very confidential," she murmured nervously.

Walters smiled. "I'll be discreet. Now, take my advice, Mrs. Dunton. This climate takes a bit of getting used to, especially when you're direct out from U.K. There's a pool at your hotel, the rooms are cool, and they mix the best gin swizzles on the Gulf. That's the place to stay until I arrive with Mark."

So she returned to the Moustafa, idled in the shade, swam lazily in the pool, and sipped tea.

When Walters arrived in the early evening he looked worried. "The odd thing is, I can't find where your husband is staying. You're sure it was Bahrain he was coming to?"

"Certain."

"I'll ring the bank tomorrow. Maybe he changed his plans, and the message didn't arrive until after you'd left. It will be some simple explanation like that. Meanwhile, why not come along to meet my wife and have a meal at the bungalow?"

She said she would rather wait until Mark surfaced.

"All right. But don't worry. I'll sort it out tomorrow, and we'll have a good laugh at whatever the muddle turns out to be."

A good laugh, she thought bitterly when he was gone. She was nearer to tears. Mark, and probably Giles with him, must have got into the place unidentified, and were lying low. But where, and for what? She had to get to him. But how? A lone woman, in a country where women didn't count, and an impossible climate. Walters would be of no help if Mark were here and in hiding, under some assumed identity.

Next day, indeed, Walters reported failure. He had phoned London. They confirmed that Mark was on a trip to Bahrain and had not notified them of any change of plan.

"Then he must be here," she insisted.

"I suppose he must," he awkwardly agreed. "It's just so odd that I can't trace him."

She gave it another three days, striving to convince

herself that in such a confined place she was bound to come across one or the other of them. She took taxi rides around the island, stopping for a while at Awali, the oil center; still inclined to think they were scheming an attack on an oil installation. But most of the time she spent in the various hotels of Manama, sitting in the lounges sipping iced coffee and reading old magazines, in the hope that one of them would happen along.

Several times a day she telephoned Walters. No news. She soon surmised that he was not making any more inquiries, convinced that she had come to the wrong place. At the end of the week he came to her hotel and told her he had booked her on a return flight to London.

"It's no use, Mrs. Dunton. Mark isn't here. I've known this for days, but until today there was one more source to tap. Now I have done that, and I can tell you he isn't in Bahrain. It's pointless for you to stay any longer. By the time you get home, your husband will probably be trying to get into touch with you in London."

She acquiesced. There was no alternative. Next day Walters drove her to the airport. As they crossed the causeway linking it to the main island, he said, "Don't worry about anything having happened to Mark, Mrs. Dunton. The whole thing must simply be a complete misunderstanding. Not only isn't he here, but he hasn't been here, or anywhere else along the Gulf."

He cosseted her through the airport lounge, ensured that she was specially looked after, and politely left. Aboard the aircraft she was at first distracted by a bunch of schoolchildren, most of them English, on their way home for the autumn school term. But they subsided as they lap-strapped themselves in and the aircraft taxied out for takeoff.

She reproached herself. It had been a panic impulse. She

had behaved like a hysterical idiot. She should have stayed in London, then Mark would have found some way of getting a message to her, a reassurance. He must have been using Bahrain as cover for his real destination. She had been trying not to accept this, but now there was no option, and her terror increased. If not here, then where? And on what horrifying mission, at what risk? She found herself quietly weeping. But she controlled that and looked out of the small porthole beside her seat as the aircraft climbed swiftly and the map of Bahrain and the Gulf unfolded below. The loudspeakers announced that seat belts could now be unfastened, and smoking was permitted. She lit a cigarette and inhaled deeply.

At that moment she became aware of a scuffle up front, then of a hostess and a steward hastening back, followed by a swarthy man; and brushed aside by another man rushing from the tail, waving a revolver and shouting, "This flight is Safad One."

He disappeared toward the flight cabin. Then from a seat near her a third man rose, a revolver in one hand, a grenade in the other, excitedly telling them all to stay in their seats, to sit quietly.

It happened so quickly that nobody instantly took it in. But then realization came. One elderly man, white-mustached, jerked impulsively up from his aisle seat, but his neighbor pulled him down. "Don't be a fool."

Another man shouted, "What's all this? Who are you?"

The man holding the steward and hostess at gunpoint replied, "Popular Front for the Liberation of Palestine."

The third man who had risen was now working down the aisle, extending a length of wire. An elderly woman seated next to Helen gripped her arm and asked in a tremulous whisper, "What's he doing?"

She answered in a calm voice, quite controlled now, even a little tensed, pleasurably, with excitement. "I think he's wiring the aircraft with explosive."

"Oh, my God!" cried the elderly woman, in tears.

Contrite, Helen soothed her. "Don't worry. They won't hurt us. It'll be all right."

But the elderly woman continued to weep silently, in fear.

A schoolboy of about ten years, beside whose seat the gunman was standing, nudged him in the leg and asked, "Is that a real gun? Honest? Show me some real bullets, won't you?"

The gunman looked nonplussed. Then suddenly several people laughed. Then everybody was laughing.

"Oh, come on," shouted a man near the front, "let's have a song. Who'll start?"

A couple of girls started, a pop song. Several of the children joined, then some of the adults. Arabs among the passengers overcame their astonishment and began to smile. An old man with a deep voice gave them "Lily of Laguna." Soon they were all roaring out old songs. The gunman let the hostess around with a tray of drinks. "On the house!" joked one man loudly. And everybody laughed. And the singing went on. Even the Arab passengers relaxed.

As the aircraft circled and dipped, it became known they were landing at Beirut. Some of the optimists thought that they would be let off there; or, at least, the women and children. It seemed there was an English diplomat in the airport tower pleading for just that. But the tower had been taken over by armed Palestinians. There would be no release.

Soon a tanker emerged across the runway and linked up to refuel the airliner. Then three more Palestinians, two men and a girl, waving guns, came running out and were hauled aboard. It all took time. On the ground, the temperature was scorching, and the air-conditioning plant not working. The singing had stopped now. Helen could feel anxiety seeping back among them all; certainly into herself. Time lagged. Nearly two hours. But then at last the tanker drove away, the engines restarted, the aircraft took off.

To get coolness back was in itself such a relief as almost to overcome the desperation of still being hostage. One of the men started singing again, and a few joined him. But it diminished. The zest for fortitude had somehow evaporated in the heat of Beirut Airport. The three new guerrillas looked unpleasant, vicious. The passengers fell silent, glum. A long line formed for the toilets.

This part of the flight, however, was little more than a hop over the mountains. As the aircraft began to circle and descend, the passengers peered from the portholes. Below was a lake of dust, through which uncertain shapes drifted. The steward's instruction to fasten seat belts was made in a steady voice. The captain brought her in beautifully, planing down through the dust, coming out into a flash of hard sunlight, with a glimpse of two other huge aircraft parked to one side.

Where were they then? At another airport?

But in a moment, as the VC-10 touched surface, bumped a little, then slid into a braked run, all of them realized that they had joined the two hijacked airliners in the Jordan desert.

"They'll let the women and children off," said one man loudly, confidently, comfortingly.

§

For Helen—and, she thought, for most of the other passengers, the women anyhow—the next forty-eight hours were misty, dreamlike. It was as though the clouds of dust that eddied in gusts across the scene, and the upward swirl of the sand devils, had penetrated her brain. She saw what was going on around her, but could no longer feel much about it.

The heat was terrifying, and little eased by the occasional dusty drafts through the open doors, where guerrillas stood guard, machine guns at the ready. For a few minutes, early in the first day, the hostages were allowed out to ease their aching muscles by walking on the baked surface of the mudflat. Parties of hostages were wandering around the two other aircraft. But there was no chance of making a run for it. Around the aircraft squatted a ring of guerrillas armed with machine guns, bazookas, mortars. Others, with weapons ready, were moving everywhere. A couple of Arabs, she saw, were straddled on the roof of the VC-10, painting a slogan in blue and red on the fuselage. Later, the aircraft's captain and a few of the passengers were taken out to give interviews to a group of newspaper reporters. Beyond, they could see the helpless squadrons of the army.

Back in the aircraft some of the passengers were organizing singsongs and party games. The children were behaving well. None panicked. For the first day they had nothing to eat except biscuits, and only tepid water to drink. But they were told the Red Cross was sending supplies of food, and next day they arrived—precooked meals, as well as medical supplies, disinfectants, diapers for the babies, and, mercifully, portable latrines.

The night was even worse than the day. The relief from heat degenerated swiftly into numbing cold. Then there was the paralysis of fear. The steward was passing on news gathered from the radio, so they knew of the threat to blow up the aircraft and everybody in it. One man, a soldier, whispered the reassurance, passed around in whispers, that the explosives positioned inside the aircraft were not fused;

so not to worry. But next day a couple of guerrillas worked slowly along the aisle, attaching detonators, and the spasms of fear returned.

Helen felt the fear, of course, but then it faded and she was no longer badly scared. Nor, she thought, was the old woman seated next to her, who had sunk into a state of calm, occasionally murmuring to herself. This dazed state was the savior. Helen scarcely knew how her mind was drifting. The hostess gave her a copy of *Homes and Gardens,* and she read and reread it, taking in the words but not the sense. She was not even worrying much about Mark any longer. For the first time in her life, she thought to herself, she understood the meaning of fatalism.

Late on the second day one of the crew told them they were to be taken to Amman. It was so sudden and unexpected that at first nobody believed it. But then a convoy of buses was seen making toward the aircraft, and there was an outbreak of laughter, cries of happiness, shouts from the children.

The first coach took away the captain, two other members of the crew, and five men passengers. Another passenger demanded from a guerrilla guard to be told where the eight had been taken, and why. But the guard roughly motioned him to join the others who were leaving the aircraft and filling the buses.

As she sat in the bus, Helen began to come alive again; with a flooding recurrence of anxiety about Mark, and of despair. But chiefly she felt weariness, intense and overwhelming weariness, and the incessant ache of her cramped muscles.

Not long after the convoy had cleared the outer ring of soldiers there were the thuds of three heavy explosions behind them.

"They've blown up the aircraft," said one of the men,

turning to look back. The glow from the flames was already mounting into the night sky.

Shortly before they reached Amman the bus stopped and an officer came on. They were now quite safe, he assured them. They would be housed overnight in the Intercontinental Hotel. Next day they would be flown from Amman to Cyprus, and then on to London. He offered them profound apologies on behalf of His Majesty King Hussein for what they had suffered in Jordan.

The Intercontinental was gleaming with lights, obviously luxurious, but with several shellholes in its front wall, smashed windows, part of the facade pockmarked by bullets. The place was crowded. It was difficult to move. Helen stood patiently waiting her turn to be taken to a room—or, as it turned out, a bed in a corridor—when she saw, standing not far off, a man she knew.

She pushed her way toward him. "Mr. Kennard."

He turned to her, astonished. "Mrs. Dunton. How on earth . . . ?"

"I was hijacked in the VC-10. I went to Bahrain to find Mark. He wasn't there." Then she understood. "He's here, isn't he?"

"He might be," Kennard awkwardly conceded.

She shook him impatiently. "Don't keep up a pretense. Where is he?"

After a long pause, Kennard took a paper from his inner breast pocket and handed it to her. "I got this from Jordan official sources this evening."

She stood reading—a report, dated two days earlier, to their superior by two men of the Camel Corps of the Desert Police. On sunset patrol they saw a jeep partly hidden in the ruins of a small hunting lodge not far from Qasr Hamman (wherever that might be, she thought). They investigated and found two armed men whom they took to be Palestinians sheltering in the ruins, where they had evidently been for several days. One of the men was lying by the wall with a bandaged leg. The response the other man made to their inquiries did not satisfy them. They told the men to get into the jeep and they would be taken to the police post at Qasr el Azraq for identification. The injured man was lifted into the back of the jeep, and the patrol told the other man to drive at their directions. But the driver shouted an order and drove off fast across the desert. The patrolmen were unslinging their rifles when the man in the rear of the jeep opened fire with an automatic weapon, killing both camels beneath them and flinging the men to the ground. By the time they could fire the jeep was distant, zigzagging; they apparently missed. Then it was out of sight. The strange fact they had to add to their report was that when the driver shouted his order, he shouted in English.

She handed the paper back to Kennard, staring at him. "Is it Mark who is wounded?"

"I think it must be. Giles is the linguist. He would be the man talking to the patrol."

"Where are they? What are they doing here?"

"I think they're probably hiding somewhere in Amman, and that they intend to assassinate a man named Yassir Arafat, the Palestinian leader."

Her hand went to her mouth. "Dear God! What can I do?"

"Nothing. Go back to London on the aircraft tomorrow."

"If Mark is here, I won't go."

"You'll have to. All British women are being evacuated. And you should go. There's nothing you can do here."

"But there is," she told him, emphatic, desperate. "Don't you see? If I can reach Mark I can stop him. I'm the only person who can, don't you see? Only find him."

Kennard paused before replying. He was assessing

possibilities. It was probably true that, if she could get to her husband, she could stop the whole thing—no violence, no bloodshed, nothing ever to be known. The chance was slight, but a chance it certainly was.

"There's nothing to be done tonight, Mrs. Dunton," he told her. "Get some sleep. I'll see tomorrow what can be arranged."

15

In spite of the zigzag course into which Giles twisted the fleeing jeep, it was hit by one rifle shot from the desert patrolmen firing from the ground where they had been thrown. But the bullet merely glanced off the side of the vehicle.

"Don't return fire," Giles shouted. "Keep your head down."

In a short while he reckoned they were out of sight, especially as the light was failing. He took a westbound track to bring him out on the Amman road. Once he had to brake, douse his lamps, and turn off the track to halt behind some scrub.

"What is it?" asked Mark.

"Patrol coming our way. Keep quiet."

It was an armored car, the commander perched high, swiveling a spotlight in a wide arc. The beam passed across the bushes and wavered. Giles was ready to make a dash. But the beam passed on.

He gave the patrol ten minutes, then resumed his drive

toward Amman. It was imperative to reach the shelter that Colonel Zouqa had offered. Holed up in the desert he had been unable to tend Mark's wound sufficiently. He needed disinfectant, pain-killers, sterilized gauze. The bullet had lodged, but Giles had probed for it with a knife and got it out. Mark took the makeshift operation in silence, fists clenched, fingernails driven into his palms. Giles sterilized the wound with the only antiseptic he had, the whiskey. It festered, of course, and for the first two days Mark ran a fever. He had come out of that now, but the leg was still swollen.

As they got nearer to Amman he could see gun flashes in the sky, and hear the rumble of artillery. Mark heard it too. "Fighting in Amman?"

"Sounds like it. I can remember the geography of the place fairly well. I was there for a time with the R.A.F. armored cars. Our best approach will be from the north, where the big refugee camps are. That'll be the side the guerrillas will be holding. It's also the easiest route to the Jebel Webdeh—Zouqa's house. We may have to force our way through. Use your revolver if possible rather than the automatics. We need to conserve ammunition. Have a couple of grenades handy."

"Okay."

"How are you feeling?"

"The wound's a bit sore. The journey hasn't helped. But I'm all right."

In the event they had luck. They came onto a network of small roads in a northern suburb where thousands of people, mostly women and children, were huddling together, having run from the refugee camps, which were taking most of the shellfire. The jeep went through that crowd almost unnoticed.

Farther in, Arafat's guerrillas were moving in large

numbers, every road crammed with ragged infantry, trucks hauling rocket launchers, trucks laden with men. The Duntons' jeep was taken for granted, never questioned.

The press of vehicles and men thinned as they drew nearer the actual combat. A few armored cars were forcing their way through the narrow, twisting streets, firing bursts into buildings and at rooftops where snipers and machine gunners were perched, or a few men with bazookas and rockets. In the distance Giles could hear the unmistakable growl of tanks. Already, in one street, corpses were huddled into the gutter and against the stucco wall of a block of flats; from inside rose the wail of women.

Twice he missed the way, but there were youths with ancient carbines crouching at street corners to redirect him. Thus he came to Zouqa's house.

It was of the older Arab kind—a tall blank wall along the road, with heavy double doors of stout timber. He found a bell rope, pulled it, but nobody came. He was contemplating an attempt to scale the wall. But then a grille in the door slowly opened.

"Qasim? You are Qasim? We are from Colonel Zouqa. He has told you we are to come."

He could barely discern the face behind the grille, though he and the jeep would be plainly visible in the moonlight; there was no street lighting anywhere in the town, he suddenly realized.

The grille closed. There came the clang of an iron bar and the big doors opened sufficiently to admit the jeep. Giles waited while the servant closed and barred the doors behind them, then asked for the stable. The servant, picking up a lantern, led them to the right through another pair of double doors. The house lay to the left around an inner courtyard, a pool, and a fountain no longer playing.

Inside the stable, which was L-shaped, long, and roomy,

stood a veteran Rolls-Royce partly shrouded by a cotton sheet, a broken cart, a Ford station wagon that looked usable, and, in one of the several horse boxes around the inner corner, a couple of bicycles. Giles put the jeep alongside the station wagon. Qasim had turned the corner into the inner part of the stable and was lifting a ladder toward the ceiling at the far end. He climbed it and opened a trap door, well concealed in the joists.

Giles followed into the loft. Qasim was lighting another lantern, although there was a swinging electric bulb. He pressed the switch to show there was no electricity. "It is the fighting. Tomorrow, perhaps."

The loft was furnished with two beds, chairs, a table, a rug on the floor. A small window in the inner wall overlooked the central courtyard, hidden from the road. It would do. Giles went down to get Mark, fireman-lifting him up the ladder and setting him down on one of the beds. He looked absolutely done in. Giles told him to forget everything and get some sleep.

He himself went down and stopped Qasim from unloading the jeep; no need to advertise the arms, even to Zouqa's servant. He gave the man some money and asked for food and water. "And has the colonel a medicine box?"

Qasim did not seem to understand. Giles motioned to lead him into the house. The rooms were small, closed up, much of the furniture stacked. In one he picked up a portable radio. In a bathroom wall cabinet he found a bottle of disinfectant, a roll of bandage, gauze. ointment, scissors.

Qasim conducted him back to the stable with his lantern, then soon returned with a tray of cooked meats, flat bread, a jug of water. When he was gone, and they had eaten, Giles cleaned up his brother's leg and redressed the wound. Suppuration was diminishing. The swelling had increased, but that was the journey. Now that he could tend the wound properly, Giles reckoned Mark should be able to get about in some fashion in a few days.

"That's much easier," Mark said, rolling over to sleep.

Giles went down to the jeep and moved everything into the loft. Then he scraped handfuls of dust from one of the stalls and flung them over the jeep itself.

Up in the loft he hoisted the ladder after him and closed the trap. The sounds of street fighting were scarcely audible in this refuge. He pulled off his clothes, treated himself to the luxury of a body-wash in a cupful of cold water, and, dousing the lantern, opened up the other bed, to sleep.

§

In the morning the guns were silent. Mark found a news bulletin on the radio. Arafat had signed a truce with the Jordan government. But already casualties in the street fighting were thought to number some four hundred. The city's power was cut off, water supply interrupted, communications severed, battles in the streets forcing people into basement shelters everywhere.

The servant arrived with coffee and bread.

"Sullen bastard," said Giles when he was gone. "I don't much like the look of him. How's the leg? Better? Good. I'll dress it again before I go."

There had to be reconnaissance. Giles went down into the courtyard and found a corridor leading to a small door in an outer wall. It was locked. He called Qasim and made him give him the key. The door opened onto a narrow alley along the side of the house. Excellent!

Now there was a truce, the streets were full of guerrillas, wandering here and there, or squatting with their guns at the positions they had been allotted, on street corners, rooftops, in some of the buildings; no sign now of the army in this part of the town. Giles moved from one group to another, squatting alongside them, gossiping, trying to pick up information. But all any of them knew was that when the time came, word would come from Abu Ammar—they always spoke of Arafat by his revolutionary name—and they would defeat the brutal Jordan army, sweep away the hated fascist Hashemite regime, turn Jordan into a people's socialist republic, and push the Jews into the sea. None had any idea where Abu Ammar was, or any contact with him; but the El Fatah headquarters was in a building at the foot of Jebel Webdeh.

Giles wandered cautiously in that direction. The building was not difficult to identify. A few guerrillas with Russian machine guns were slouching outside it, but the guard was slack. Once Mark was mobile, Giles felt sure they could get in there without much trouble, and out again if they held a vital hostage. But after he had covertly watched for a while, he became convinced that it was not there that Arafat was hiding. The place wasn't busy enough to house the commander.

When he got back to the stable, Mark told him that he had managed to walk a few steps without a stick, and without too much pain.

"Good. Keep at it. Anything on the radio useful to us?"

"No," said Mark. "Only general stuff. There's a hell of a row going on about the aircraft hostages still held, and the girl hijacker still in a London police station. The Yanks are moving the Sixth Fleet closer, and there are reports of U.S. Air Force fighters gathering in Turkey. Did you get anything?"

Giles shook his head. "Nothing much. There's an El Fatah H.Q. at the bottom of this hill, but I'm sure Arafat isn't there."

Mark switched on the radio and fiddled with it until he got the El Fatah transmitter. "It can't be far off," he said. "Listen how loud we're getting it—and I bet it's only a weak, portable machine."

With that Giles agreed. "So far as I can make out, we're near the fringe of the districts held by the guerrillas. North of here, every street is thick with them. My guess is that he's holed up somewhere between us and the nearest refugee camp on the outskirts. Maybe I'll come across some clue to the exact place, if I keep on reconnoitering."

But every day he returned from his sortie less and less hopeful.

"I'm pretty sure I've pinned him down to an area not far from here, higher up the hill. Every time I wander that way, I get questioned too closely, so I have to turn back."

"So what?"

"So we wait," answered Giles. "What else? It's this damn truce. While it lasts, there's nothing to bring him out into the open. But it won't last. When the fighting starts again, he'll have to surface. He's the commander-in-chief."

Each day, while Giles was on his reconnaissance, Mark exercised his leg to the limit. Within three days he was walking round the loft with fair ease. He would not allow the onset of pain to check him. His sole objective now was to get fit enough to join in the attack as soon as the opportunity occurred. Get the damn thing finished. Now that they were actually in the field, he wanted action.

On the fourth morning he managed to get down the ladder, awkward though it was with his wounded leg stiff. He walked slowly for a while around the stable, then moved toward the inner courtyard.

What checked him was the sound of voices in the house. He moved in slowly, silently.

The door to a rear room was ajar. Qasim the servant was

seated with three men in El Fatah dress, fully armed. They were doing the talking, Qasim listening. Mark could make out only scraps of it, but what he could understand was enough. He moved away as silently as he had come, climbed the ladder, pulled it up after him, and sat by the open trap, waiting to lower it when Giles returned.

"What's up?" asked Giles.

"I went downstairs. Qasim was getting orders from three guerrillas. He is to lead them to the target tomorrow night. We're the target."

"How could they have known?"

"Presumably from Qasim himself. He's probably en-rolled. It's the usual way—the servants of the Establish-ment are secret revolutionaries. He must know we're not Arabs. He has heard us talking. The assumption is that we're some sort of spies. So he reports to his commander, and they'll come to get us."

"Tomorrow night," mused Giles. "I suppose it'll be when he brings the supper. The others come behind him with guns and take us by surprise."

"Do we get out tonight?"

"No. We'll have to move, of course. But we'd better deal with this little local difficulty first."

16

The authorities wanted to fly Helen Dunton out of Jordan with the other released hostages. Roy Chapman, briefed by Kennard, therefore had a quiet argument with the right man at the embassy, who at last reluctantly agreed. "But keep the woman out of sight as much as possible for a few days."

Kennard told her she would have to share their room. She could have the bed in the alcove. He would rig up a sheet as screen. At that she smiled wanly, indifferent to anything except Mark's safety. Through the days of the truce she sat most of the time on the small balcony, a radio by her side, catching every bulletin in English.

After the ferocity of those twenty-four hours in Amman, the truce was an immense relief, of course. But it was of little use to Kennard. He had no hope of penetrating any part of the city north of the central valley. All those districts were firmly held by the guerrillas; and it was there that the Duntons were almost certainly crouched. Even if he knew exactly where they were, he doubted if he could reach them.

Ned Bartholomew declared cheerfully that it no longer mattered. He had seen, at the U.S. embassy, a detailed report on the Amman situation. Arafat was still in the city, though his exact location was unknown. He was lodged with a botched-up radio transmitter, somewhere between Jebel Webdeh and the refugee camps on the northern outskirts.

What was known was that he was surrounded by a picked guard armed with machine guns, bazookas, grenades, and mortars—virtually impenetrable, except by armor.

"The Duntons will never get anywhere near him. We have to go through the motions, of course, but it's all a waste of time."

That dismissed the subject for Bartholomew. He went on to tell them amusingly of an American college kid he had picked up.

"Here's this kid, living at the Y.W.C.A., just round the corner from here, wandering about by herself in the middle of all this screaming hell, quite unperturbed. I tell you, it's refreshing. What do you think she said to me? She said she was having a wonderful vacation, and it was all a great experience, and *fun*. How about that?"

Kennard made no comment. He was remembering the women and children fleeing from the artillery battle at Irbid, and the corpses already festering in the side streets of Amman, cleared away by nobody. How many more might there be if Giles Dunton actually succeeded in getting Arafat?

§

The end of the truce was abrupt.

Heavy fighting started in north Jordan. The civilian government resigned. The King went on the air to announce a military government and martial law. By implication, the army had at last been given the go-ahead.

Kennard stood anxiously by Miller, who translated briefly the Arabic broadcast as it went along.

"So now?" asked Kennard.

"Now there'll be an inevitable response from El Fatah."

Miller was sliding the radio tuner, at last getting the underground wavelength. A man was shouting fiercely.

"Arafat himself," said Chapman.

"What's he saying?"

Miller resumed as interpreter. "He's calling on all Palestinians to overthrow Hussein and his regime. . . . He's ordering his men to stand by with their finger on the trigger."

The broadcast ended in a wail of music, then a stream of vituperation.

Miller switched off. "It can't be long now."

Almost as he said it came the rumble of heavy artillery from the outskirts. The three men moved onto the balcony.

Miller pointed. "Tanks coming in from the west."

Kennard turned his gaze. "And guerrillas swarming in from the north."

Already the tanks were opening up. Already bazookas were launching at them from rooftops.

"In those narrow streets they'll be sitting ducks," said Miller.

"They'll come through," Chapman confidently answered. "They're Bedouin, and they've been aching for this for months."

Within minutes, indeed, the leading armored cars were emerging onto the streets of Jebel Amman, all around the hotel, and tanks were grinding up the slopes. At the same time guerrillas were rushing into all the buildings, lugging bazookas onto the roofs.

At every rocket salvo or burst of machine-gun fire, the armor responded with point-blank shelling. There were snipers and machine gunners on the roof of the hotel itself, and immediately the guns opened up on them, smashing first the penthouse nightclub, then switching to blast holes in a block of flats nearby.

Kennard watched grimly, and Chapman appreciatively, as guerrillas firing from the windows of the flats were forced upward by shellfire, story by story, until their last bazooka, hauled onto the roof, was destroyed by a shell. Then came a squad of infantry, bursting into the entrance to the block, mopping up with small arms, flinging the bodies of the guerrillas from the windows, to sprawl, grotesquely broken, on the roadway.

A raking of machine-gun bullets came spurting across the hotel face. The three men ducked into the room, Kennard pulling Helen Dunton to safety. The windows were shattered by a stray volley. A hotel porter was running along the corridors, shouting, "Down to the basement shelters. Down to the basement for shelter."

"Not yet," muttered Kennard.

He was looking cautiously through the smashed windows. Thick pillars of smoke were rising on hilltops to the north where the refugee camps lay, and fires were starting in the city center. But the tanks were not making much progress. In several places they were held, with battles raging round them.

A bullet ricocheted from the balcony pillar into the room, burying itself in the inner wall. Kennard dragged a mattress into the corridor and made Helen take refuge there; she refused to go to the basement.

But by nightfall they all had to go down. The fighting was now intense. All over the city tall fires were leaping. Near at hand, groups of guerrillas were darting into the hotel, firing at troops and armored cars outside, then slipping away as the return fire came. The din was incessant.

The basement was suffocatingly full. To the hotel guests, including about a hundred newspaper and television correspondents, were added people who had been caught in the street, or had taken refuge from nearby apartments and villas which had been seized by the Palestinians and were being hammered by tanks and armored cars. Lanterns gave the only light, for the electricity supply had been cut. So had the water supply; there was none except that already stored in the hotel's cisterns. Water and food rationing was being prepared. The battle above might last for days.

"Nonsense," maintained Chapman. "The army will clear out that rabble in hours."

Kennard dissented. The guerrillas were either fanatics or dupes. They could not win, but they could die in their thousands, losing.

§

There were lulls in the fighting, but it went on and on. During daylight hours, people in the hotel moved up from the basement, sometimes to be pinned down on the corridor floors by sniper fire and the inevitable retaliation. None could venture outside the hotel itself. The military had imposed a total curfew and warned that anybody appearing on the streets would be shot. For three days the only link with outside was the radio, giving equal cover to the massacre in Amman and to the quest for fifty-four hostages still held by the Palestinians, presumably somewhere in the middle of all this turmoil.

Peering cautiously from time to time from the window of his room, Kennard despaired. Over the whole city rolled thick clouds of black smoke. In the distance mortars were smashing at buildings from which guerrillas were blazing with automatic fire. Near the hotel, where the army was gaining control, ambulances were touring the streets, calling through loudspeakers to the wounded to come out and be taken to the hospital: "Give yourselves up. You will be treated with the honor of a brother."

But few stirred. Most of the ambulances went empty through streets strewn with corpses lying in dried pools of their own blood.

On the fourth day the curfew was lifted for three hours, so that women could leave their homes and search for food. Several foreigners who had been pinned down in blocks of flats or in smaller hotels seized the chance to move hastily across to the Intercontinental.

Kennard was standing by the hotel entrance when he saw Ned Bartholomew approaching, with a girl in a ragged shawl and long skirt.

Bartholomew brought her up to him. "God, the time we've had! This is Shirle, the American college kid I told you about. I got her out of the Y.W., but before I could bring her here all hell broke loose. We ran for the nearest shelter, a block of flats, and found an inside bathroom. The apartment was empty except for a dead dog in the front room. I tossed it into the street. There was food in the kitchen, and bottles of lemonade. So we lived. But am I glad to get here!"

The girl was far less shaken than he. She smiled cheerfully at Kennard. "Some vacation I'm having!"

There was the snap of a sniper bullet. A soldier standing near the entrance fell.

Kennard grabbed the girl and pulled her inside, Bartholomew flopping to the floor beside them. People outside the entrance were running for cover as Saladins and Saracens only twenty yards away opened fire on the building from which the sniper's shot had come. Shells smashed the front wall. Half a dozen infantrymen, machine guns ready, ran crouching across the street and into the building. A hysterical woman rushed from its front entrance, tearing at her hair and wailing. The soldiers ignored her. From the interior came the rattle of their guns.

"Come on up to our room," said Kennard, rising. "There's an internal bathroom for shelter if firing starts again."

Chapman, Miller, and Helen Dunton were already there. Shirle greeted them happily. "Hi!"

Bartholomew said, "Listen. She knows Giles Dunton. She has seen him in Jordan."

Kennard stared.

"Well, I think I have," said Shirle. "He was in the ship from Marseilles to Beirut. We were together a lot. He bought me lunch at that big hotel in Beirut, then I left him. But I thought I saw him again, dressed like an Arab. I can't be sure. The funny thing was, the man I saw was talking their Arab language. But if it wasn't Giles, it was the nearest likeness I ever did see."

"Where?" asked Kennard.

Bartholomew answered. "In the house of a Colonel Zouqa, somewhere in the country up north, near Jerash."

Kennard grimaced. "Interesting, but now academic."

Helen seized Shirle's arm. "Was there another man with him?"

"Sure. There were two, dressed like Arabs."

"Was the other one wounded—hurt in any way?"

"Not that I noticed," said Shirle.

Roy Chapman interrupted. "Wait a minute. There's still a possibility. I know Colonel Zouqa slightly. He used to be in the palace. He's from one of the older families that moved into Amman when Abdullah picked on it as his capital after the First World War, and began to build it up. Most of them still have the town houses they built then, as well as farms in the country."

§

Miller was already grabbing for the telephone directory on the bedside table, thumbing it. "Zouqa . . . Zouqa . . . Colonel Abdul Zouqa."

"That's the one," said Chapman, reaching for the directory. "Ah, the house isn't far—over there, across the valley. It's on the slope of Jebel Webdeh."

Kennard went down and into the street, fast, seeking an officer. "Do you speak English? Good. I have to get to this address without delay. It's official business."

"Official?"

Kennard handed him the authority which Badir had signed. The officer read it with surprise, then shouted, and a senior officer walked over.

"I have to get to this house," Kennard repeated. "It's official business, and very important. I have a car which can be brought round from the hotel garage. There will be a driver, myself, and one other."

The officer read the paper, took in the insignia and the signature, and asked, "What do you need?"

"An escort to the house and, soon afterward, back here again."

"You know the risk? There are snipers infiltrating even into areas we have already cleared. I can give no guarantee of a safe journey."

Kennard nodded. "Understood. We'll be ready, here, in ten minutes."

When Miller brought the car round, a Saladin was waiting ahead of it. Then Kennard came out with Helen. The officer gaped. "A woman?"

"Get going," said Kennard abruptly.

There was less trouble on the way than he had feared. Only once did a sniper fire at them, from a rooftop. The Saladin's gun swung instantly, there was a quick burst, then silence. Whether the man had been hit, Kennard could not tell.

In some streets he was startled by the devastation—substantial buildings smashed, the interiors collapsed. There must be hundreds of corpses in the rubble. In places the sickly stench of putrefaction was almost unbearable.

The street on the slope of the Jebel Webdeh on which the armored car halted was, however, deserted, and seemed quiet. The house to which the officer pointed was a blank wall with large double doors. Did he want them smashed open?

But Miller was already exploring a side alley. "There's a small door here unfastened."

Kennard told the officer, "We'll go in that way. If men come out through these main doors, grab them, but don't kill them. They're wanted alive. But I should warn you they're well armed, and dangerous."

Kennard led through the side door, then Helen, then Miller. They were unarmed. "No guns," Kennard had ordered. "That's not the exercise."

A passage led to a courtyard around a disused fountain. There was complete silence. Gesturing to the others to remain where they were, Kennard moved cautiously around the yard and into the rooms beyond.

In most of them the furniture was stacked, the rugs rolled. In one, a sort of kitchen, used food plates stood on the wooden table, and a half-empty jug of wine. There was nobody in any of the rooms.

He emerged again into the yard. To his right a wide entrance passage led to the main doors, which were heavily barred. On the far side of the passage was another set of double doors. They were open. Obviously the garage, which had probably in older times been the house stable.

Kennard peered around the door post of the stable entrance. A vintage Rolls-Royce standing on blocks and partly covered by a sheet; a Ford station wagon; a dusty jeep.

The stable was L-shaped. Along the rear wall ran the old stalls and mangers. Kennard moved to the corner past the jeep and edged around it until he could look down the length of the other leg of the stable.

Near the far end a ladder led to an open trap door in the ceiling. At its foot sprawled three bodies.

Kennard moved closer. Two were men in the usual guerrilla dress. They were not the Duntons. They had been shot from behind. The machine guns they must have been holding had fallen clear of them. The third body was dressed in a caftan. From the tray of food scattered on the floor beside him, he had been a servant.

Kennard stepped carefully over the bodies and got his foot on the ladder, hauling himself onto it as gently as he could, fearful lest it creak. When he was halfway up, it creaked. There was nothing for it but to go steadily on.

He bit his lip and raised his head above the entrance to the loft. It was furnished like a living room. The two beds had been used and were unmade. A soiled bandage lay crumpled on the floor beside a bowl of fluid. On the table stood an empty whiskey bottle.

They had been there, of course. They had somehow survived an ambush. And they were gone.

17

Giles had already decided upon their next refuge, once they had dealt with the ambush in the stable.

That had not been difficult. Half an hour before Qasim regularly brought supper each evening, Giles took his Browning automatic pistol and hid in the rear of the ancient Rolls-Royce, scratching with his finger a tiny peephole in the dust that covered its windows. Qasim came with the tray of food, followed by two guerrillas with unslung machine guns.

When they had turned the corner, Giles emerged quietly from the Rolls-Royce, ran to the stable entrance to make sure there was no rear guard, then back to the corner of the wall. By the time he reached it, all three were on the ladder, Qasim nearly at the trap.

One burst from his Browning brought down all three. He slipped in a fresh magazine, stepped across, and put it into them again, to make sure; then shouted to Mark to come down.

The jeep was to be left in the stable for their getaway. Giles had already packed, into two sacks he found in the stable, as many grenades as they could carry, all the reserve ammunition, and a couple of smoke canisters. He went up to the loft to collect the sacks, and a couple of blankets into which he had rolled two mugs, a bottle of water, several knives, and the radio. Into one of the sacks he emptied the loaf and slices of meat from Qasim's supper tray. He slung the lot on the two bicycles that stood in the stable.

They left through the small side door, leaving it unlocked; they might want to get back through it in a hurry. Mark had some difficulty getting onto his bicycle saddle, but Giles helped him up and then he could move quite well, using only one pedal. It was the day the truce was broken, and battle was engaged all around, fiercest a little farther down the slope of the hill.

Leading the way, Giles turned up a slight slope. At the second road junction he halted in the shadow of a wall, dismounted, and grasped Mark's handlebars to hold him steady. The street ahead was like a gallery overlooking the main battle on the Jebel Webdeh. The lower side was cleared of buildings, and guerrillas were straddled there behind a low stone wall, firing bursts at infantry scurrying on the slopes below. On the other side of the street, where several buildings were still standing, rocket launchers were crouched in their shelter, and on the roofs. They were letting go at two tanks and three armored cars some way down the hill. Return fire from the tanks was crumbling the walls. Occasionally, too, there were bursting shells from heavy batteries stationed far off to the southeast.

The nearest guerrilla machine gunner, seeing them, rose as though to approach. Giles shouted to him. He gestured his indifference and dropped back into cover.

"We've got to get into the shelter of that building at the

far end," said Giles. "Wait for a salvo from the heavies. Then I'll shove you off. Make it as fast as you can."

There were six successive shellbursts. The largest guerrilla rocket post was hit, the bodies flung outward into the road. Halfway along, the front of a house thundered into rubble.

"Now," ordered Giles, thrusting Mark's machine off; jumping on his own and pedaling after it, crouched as low as he could get.

A shell from one of the tanks exploded against a wall just after they passed, the splinters screaming. The impact swerved him almost into a spill. But he recovered and kept going. Then they were both in the shelter of the building, gasping, Mark's face strained with the pain from his leg.

Breathless, Giles said, "We can take it easier now. Up there, just past the Caravan Hotel, there's a small street turning left. Twenty yards up that street is a burned-out garage. That's our hide. Can you make it? All right, let's go."

Behind what remained of the garage wall he helped Mark to dismount and descend some broken steps into a cellar. He brought down the sacks, the blanket rolls, and the bicycles, item by item, and closed a trap door in the floor above.

The only light was moonlight and the flare of battle, piercing into the cellar from a shell cavity at the far end.

"There's a tap from a cistern upstairs that miraculously has only the top half broken, so we have some water. For food we have two loaves and the supper meat. We'll have to ration until I can forage."

"Then what?"

"We wait until the man surfaces. He's bound to. He may have already. With luck, we'll get a tip from the radio. If the luck holds, we'll be in approximately the right position. His hideout is somewhere on this hill, I'm sure of that. By the guerrilla dispositions round here, it's my guess we could be quite close."

§

The curfew that had been lifted for a few hours was soon slammed down again. Guerrillas were infiltrating back at night into districts that the army had cleared by day. Street battles resumed in the glow of numerous fires in the city and the unclouded strength of the full moon, filtered only by drifting columns of smoke.

Kennard spent a lot of time in the hotel room, trying to align his mind with the thinking of Giles Dunton, trying to anticipate how and where he would act.

He started to narrow possibilities. With one wounded, the brothers could not have gone far. They were probably still on Jebel Webdeh, holed up somewhere. Dunton would recognize the impossibility of getting into Arafat's heavily guarded headquarters. So he must wait until Arafat emerged on the streets. How would he know?

Kennard lowered his eyes and stared absently at Helen, sitting on the other side of the room in the alcove that sheltered her from a sniper's chance bullet, listening to a World Service news bulletin.

Then he sat up. That was it. That was how Giles would know. The radio.

At that moment Kennard was certain, with the certainty of one of his hunches, that the Duntons were lying hidden in the center of the city, listening to the radio for the tip that Arafat was moving, and where.

Kennard went across to Miller and gave his reasoning.

"I can cover the bulletins in English myself, of course," Kennard told him. "But Giles will be getting the Arabic ones too—much more likely to give him the information he needs. That means you and Chapman. Work out a roster of watches, from before dawn until after midnight. Tell me if there's even a hint of Arafat's movements. If I'm asleep, wake me." He paused. Suppose it were at night; it was most likely to be at night. "Tell Chapman to bring dark clothing for us all—black jeans and slacks, sweaters and caps. Tell him to bring a couple of automatics too. We may need them as well as our own guns."

Miller gave a grunt of satisfaction. That made better sense.

So the operation resolved itself into a radio-monitoring service. On one wavelength the army was claiming control of most of Amman; on another, the Palestine Red Crescent was appealing to the International Red Cross to succor Amman, "now a blazing inferno." Arafat's underground transmitter was calling on all Arab countries to come to the Palestinians' aid; not long after, Syrian tanks crossed the frontier into Jordan in strength, and major battles were developing in the north.

Damascus was howling against the King and the Hashemite butchers, and the "terrible massacre, the like of which history has never witnessed." One broadcast gave the text of Arafat's appeal to Nasser of Egypt: "Amman is burning for the sixth day. Thousands of our people are under the debris. Bodies have rotted. . . . Hunger and thirst are killing our remaining children, women and old men. . . . A sea of blood and twenty thousand killed and wounded separate the Palestinians from Jordan's army. . . ."

"Any hint at all of where he's speaking from?" asked Kennard.

Miller shook his head. "None."

Even the Jordan authorities, it seemed, did not know. The radio reported King Hussein's press conference at Hummar, his country house a few miles outside the capital; he chiefly wanted to announce that the Syrians were getting a bloody nose, a thumping, and were being driven back in disorder. The King was asked where Yassir Arafat was. He replied that he did not know. There had been many attempts to contact him, to ensure his safety, "but we haven't found him, though we believe he is still in the area."

"Damn," muttered Kennard. "Damn, damn, damn!" He looked at his men in frustration. "Should we go over to Jebel Webdeh tonight on the off chance?"

"Policy of desperation," said Miller shortly.

Kennard had to agree.

"Also needless," put in Bartholomew, who had come up from the basement, where he had left the American girl. He had thought of taking her to the U.S. embassy. "But it stands on Jebel Webdeh," he said, "in the combat area. You can get in or out only in an armored car. Can you imagine that your fellows have a chance of getting within even sniping distance of Arafat? Baloney! Keep your cool and quit worrying."

§

In the darkest corner of the garage cellar, behind a screen of old boxes and other junk, Giles lay on his blanket alongside his brother, listening to the latest radio bulletin from Damascus. But it told him nothing of Arafat.

He raised himself to open the third of five cans of fish he had found, together with a tin of hard biscuits, on one of his reconnaissance forays, in a shelled, looted grocery store nearby. It was what they now had to live on. He had stopped reconnaissance. One or two of the guerrillas to whom he had casually chatted once or twice were starting to look at him with a hint of suspicion. So he stayed in the garage.

He felt Mark's hand grip his arm, cautionary. Giles turned his head. There was a slight noise on the far side of the screen of boxes. Somebody was in the cellar.

Giles moved slowly and silently, loosing his revolver from his belt.

Around the corner of the screen wandered an Arab boy. He halted, scared, when he saw them. Giles shot him between the eyes; there was a look of astonishment on his face even as he fell.

Mark muttered a reproach, but Giles ignored it. They could not take even the slightest risk. He dragged the boy's body to the end of the cellar and dumped it just outside the gaping hole where the shells had struck. The flies fastened greedily on it. Before long it would stink. All the better, Giles said grimly to himself; an added indication to anybody who was curious that there was nobody in the cellar.

He went back to his place behind the boxes and turned the radio even lower; it might have been that that had attracted the intruder. But listen he must. It was now his only source.

The break came on the last Thursday of that month of September; announcement over the radio that a peace mission was flying to Amman from Cairo, led by General Nimeiry, the President of the Sudan, representing the heads of Arab states gathered in summit with Nasser of Egypt.

Nimeiry appealed on the radio to Arafat. "Say where you are, brother. Say how you can be reached."

Giles turned to his brother. "This will be it. If they're going to talk by radio there's bound to be a direction, a place of meeting. We may not get much warning. We may have to move fast, though my guess is that it won't be far. Can you make it, Mark? Is the leg strong enough?"

"It'll do."

18

Kennard reacted with equal certainty when Miller translated the Nimeiry broadcast.

"This is it. This'll be the one chance they have of knowing where Arafat is."

"Suppose he doesn't respond," argued Miller. "Or suppose the meeting is fixed by messenger?"

"Then I'll agree with Bartholomew that the Duntons have failed and we can pick them up with fair ease when the fighting stops. Let's hope so. But don't miss a minute of the underground radio, either of you. If Arafat does respond, that'll be it. We'll have to move fast."

Helen came over. "When you move, I'm coming with you."

"Not this time," Kennard said.

"You're taking guns?"

"Yes, we're taking guns."

Her voice was pleading. "Give me one last try to stop them. I know I can."

"Mrs. Dunton, you have to face facts. You're not coming with us. You would be an embarrassment on the way, and useless if you got there. The time for persuasion is past. Now we have to take guns."

She stared at him for a moment. "Yes," she admitted at last, "I must face facts. You are right."

She returned to the alcove and lay on her bed.

Kennard sat down by Miller at the radio. "Don't miss it. When's Chapman due?"

"In about an hour."

"Hope he's in time."

But when Chapman arrived there had been no response from Arafat. Nor was there any throughout the day. The hours crawled by. Kennard was picturing to himself Giles Dunton, crouched similarly over a radio, waiting as tensely, somewhere within a couple of miles, but beyond reach.

By nightfall there was still no response.

"We'll change," Kennard decided, "just in case."

The two others looked skeptical, but of course obeyed. They put on the black sweaters and dark slacks. The three black knitted balaclavas were set out on one of the beds. Miller was burning a cork with which they blackened each other's faces; nobody made jokes. Then they turned back to the radio.

Still there was nothing. Hour after weary hour—nothing.

"By midnight we should give it up," suggested Miller.

Kennard made no reply.

But shortly before midnight Chapman gripped Kennard by the arm. Miller, on watch, began to translate.

"'A message from Abu Ammar to His Excellency General Jafaar al-Nimeiry. A message from Abu Ammar to His Excellency General Jafaar al-Nimeiry. . .' They're repeating it over and over."

"They're giving time for somebody to warn him to listen," said Kennard. "Stay with it."

Miller sat silent, listening; then stiffened.

"'Here is the message. Drive in your cars along the road which leads from the Caravan Hotel to the Egyptian embassy, across Jebel Webdeh. We have asked our forces on Jebel Webdeh to ensure your safe arrival and not to interfere with your cars. Your brother Abu Ammar. I will repeat this message. Abu Ammar to His Excellency General Jafaar al-Nimeiry. Drive in your cars. . . .'"

Kennard was already fixing a holster.

Chapman took a street map from the table. "The road from the Caravan Hotel is this one. At the western end there has been almost complete devastation. It can't be there. At the other end, as it nears the Egyptian embassy, the guerrillas are no longer in control, except in isolated pockets. Arafat could be cut off in one of those, but it's unlikely. In between there's this stretch of road across Jebel Webdeh. The meeting must be somewhere there, surely."

"How do we get there?"

"Commandeer an armored car," suggested Miller.

Kennard dissented. "No good. They wouldn't come, even on Badir's authority. Not there, not tonight. Even if we could con one of them into taking us, it would be risking too much. If we were wrong, and we interfered with the Nimeiry meeting, we might have wrecked the whole chance of stopping the fighting. It must be on foot."

"Then it's down here in the valley," said Chapman, drawing his finger across the map, "and up this slope here. I know a few back ways, but it will be tricky."

They went down to the basement and out through the hotel garage and a back entrance. On the way they collected the automatics which Miller had locked into the car.

In one way the bright moonlight was a difficulty, for they could not keep continually in black shadows. But it did help Chapman pick out the route.

At first they were in hazard from the army. Most of the

district had been cleared of guerrillas. In one or two streets there was sporadic fire. Down one there was a rocket flash from a rooftop, then a Saladin firing rapidly at the building from which it had come, and steel-helmeted infantrymen slipping across the road one by one, then opening up with automatics as they thrust into the entrance.

There were army patrols too near for comfort. Once they had to stand flat against a darkened wall, waiting for a Saladin to pass. They realized they had nearly walked into a command post. They silently took another road.

Shortly afterward Miller whispered, "We're being followed."

Kennard said, "You two go on, but slowly."

He stepped into a darkened doorway and waited.

In a couple of minutes he heard a faint footfall. He counted two, then grabbed.

She gave a small scream, stifling it quickly.

"Mrs. Dunton," he whispered angrily. "Of all the damn fool things—"

"You can't take me back now. You haven't time."

§

Kennard saw the two others sidling back in the shadow of the wall. They stopped, staring at her. She too had put on a black sweater and slacks; she must have gotten them from the Red Cross handout. She too had corked her face. Her hair was tucked into a beret.

"She'll have to come," Kennard muttered.

"But dammit . . . " protested Miller.

"Keep your voices down," whispered Chapman. "And come on. We've got to get going."

Kennard jerked his thumb and they went ahead,

Chapman leading, Kennard in the middle with the woman, Miller in the rear.

Once across the valley they started up the lower slope of Jebel Webdeh. Suddenly around the corner swung an armored car. It pulled up to halt them, the gunner swinging.

"Tell him we're official," said Kennard quickly, handing to Chapman the Badir authority—crumpled and soiled by now, but still legible.

The car commander read it by the light of a torch, then handed it back. Chapman talked quickly to him. The officer answered volubly, gesturing up the hill. Although he kept his voice low, he was clearly audible. Kennard realized that there was near-silence. The guns had ceased. The peace mission must have started.

The armored car drove on.

"It was useful," Chapman told Kennard. "There's a guerrilla strongpoint a little further up this road, but he gave me a way round. Clear at the moment, he said, but be quick, they have patrols out."

The way led up footpaths rising almost precipitously up the rocky slopes between the contour roadways. At one point they were climbing. The woman couldn't make it. Kennard had to haul her up.

Chapman halted at last in the shadow of a small ruined house. He pointed to the west. "The meeting should be somewhere along that stretch of road. I think there are guards squatting behind the walls on either side."

Kennard nodded. "There's a machine-gun post in a building on the lower side of the road, facing down the valley. I suppose we could manage from here. But if it were possible to get nearer . . . See that alley coming down to the road, from behind, about a hundred yards along? There's a pile of rubble up there which ought to give a field of fire over most of the roadway. Is it possible to get there? I can't see any guards on that side. It's their interior side, of course."

"Machine gunner on the roof of the corner house," murmured Miller.

Chapman was studying the ground, lit still by the brightness of the setting moon, casting impenetrable black shadows behind every building.

"There is a path," he whispered, "running behind that low wall. There's one road gap we'll have to get across singly. . . . It's just possible."

"Let's go."

Chapman went across the moonlit gap first, swiftly and silently. Kennard waited to make sure he had not attracted attention, then whispered to the woman, "You next."

He heard her suck in her breath sharply, but she gave no other sign of fear. She went across the gap perfectly. Kennard followed. They waited. Miller did not come.

Then Kennard saw a guerrilla patrolling the road below, looking up at the gap, alerted. He raised his machine gun and put a burst across the area. The rooftop machine gunner came quickly to his parapet. Both men stood there for several minutes. Then the man on the roof shouted something to his comrade on the ground. Apparently satisfied, the patrolman went on. The man on the roof returned to his gun position.

Miller came quickly across. "Everybody all right?"

"Sure."

Chapman, crouching, was moving cautiously now behind the low wall.

"Watch your feet," he whispered back. "Lots of loose stone."

Kennard motioned to the woman to follow. When he was satisfied that she was keeping under cover, moving well, he himself started, unable to check her any longer, fully occupied guarding his own footsteps and keeping low enough.

He reached the heap of rubble. Chapman and the woman were squatting behind it. He peered over the top. It was only a few yards higher than the roadway—close enough to hear the murmur of two guards, somewhere down there, talking to each other.

By pointing, he placed Chapman and Miller, prone, side by side on the lip of the rubble heap, their automatics poised. He made the woman lie hidden beside them. She edged up so that she too could see into the road. He shrugged and let her be.

"Now listen," he ordered, keeping his voice low, "nobody moves from this position. If we have to fire, it must be single shots—and don't miss. There will certainly be shooting down below, if we do have to fire, so our position isn't likely to be spotted. Whatever happens, we stay here until I give the word to withdraw. Then we go back the way we came. Understood?"

After the grunts of assent he took up position on the lip, between the two men.

Miller nudged him and pointed away to the west. Car headlights were wavering over the crest of the hill. "Nimeiry."

Soon Kennard could see that there were only two cars. Since Nimeiry's mission numbered eight men, they must be coming unescorted, trusting to Arafat's radio promise that his forces on Jebel Webdeh would not fire on the cars, or interfere.

The cars were moving slowly, doubtless because the drivers were twisting their way along shell-pitted roads.

"They're just passing the Caravan Hotel now," whispered Chapman. "They should be here in about ten minutes."

He swiveled his glance, then touched Kennard's arm. Some half a dozen guerrillas had emerged from the house that had the machine gunner on the roof.

"Could be the meeting place."

The moonlight was still sufficient for the group in the roadway to be seen with partial clarity. They were standing around a short, rather stout Arab, as it might be their leader. As it might be Arafat, Kennard whispered to himself. As it might be . . . At that distance, in that light, he could not be sure.

The cars were nearer now. They disappeared behind a line of buildings, then came into view on the open stretch of the road.

A few guerrillas were running alongside the cars as escort. Two of them, on bicycles, were well ahead of the small convoy.

The men who had emerged from the house were moving toward the middle of the road.

Kennard was gazing at the two cyclists, who put on speed and drew farther ahead of the cars.

"One of them's lame," he murmured, "using only one pedal. Good God!"

The lame cyclist had flung himself from his machine onto the ground, firing a machine-gun burst that hit the gunner on the roof and thrust his body over the parapet to plunge down to the road.

The other cyclist was racing ahead, one arm swinging as he hurled a canister from which smoke spurted.

The guerrillas in the road were recoiling, startled, in terror. Two or three had fallen. There was a smatter of gunfire.

Kennard pushed out his automatic. The men beside him raised theirs.

"Single shots."

But then he cried abruptly to stop.

The woman was running down the rough slope below, shouting, "Mark! Mark!"

The cyclist on the ground jerked round sharply, holding his fire, gazing up.

The other cyclist was dismounted now, running forward, firing as he ran, but twisting his head around and shouting, "Cover. Cover, man. Cover."

At that instant the woman was hit. She jerked backward, gave a cry, pitched over.

The man on the ground sprang for the roadside, racing toward her swiftly, for all his limp.

He reached her at the same time as Kennard, running from above; the two others close behind.

Back on the road there was a sharp burst of fire, then another. Mark Dunton turned and threw a canister, and smoke surged across the roadway, choking, blinding, joining the smoke his brother had flung.

Kennard had already lifted the woman.

"Follow me," ordered Mark, making sharply left and leading fast across the slope.

At the first road he mounted the hill for a few yards, then turned into a small street, and down an alley.

Kennard could take the burden no longer. Miller lifted her from him, and they ran on. Mark was leading them through a small door in a high wall, slamming it behind them.

In a moment Kennard realized they were in Colonel Zouqa's house. Mark was already in the stable, starting the jeep motor. Miller climbed on the back with the woman in his arms.

Chapman, at a nod from Mark, lifted the iron bars from the wide front doors, tugging them open, then jumping up behind on the jeep.

Kennard clambered into the seat beside Mark. "Where are you going?"

"Making for the desert."

Kennard pushed the muzzle of his revolver into Mark's side. "Don't be a bloody fool. Don't you want your wife to have a chance? Down into the valley and across to the Intercontinental. If we come to an army patrol, pull up. Keep your headlamps on, no matter what. If you go into a ditch they'll have the lot of us."

19

In his room at the Intercontinental Hotel Kennard switched on the radio. It was relatively quiet outside now, no gunfire except distantly, in the center of the city where small groups of guerrillas were still active.

They listened to the news bulletin. Arafat and Nimeiry had flown from Amman to Cairo in the early hours of the morning. Hussein would follow. Both sides had agreed on a cease-fire. In a few days there would be a peace treaty. For the present, the horror was ending.

Sixteen of the missing hostages had been found in Wahdat refugee camp, where they had survived days and nights of shellfire. The peace talks at the United Nations had been suspended. Diplomatic sources thought it unlikely they would be resumed.

Kennard leaned forward to switch it off.

"I heard an hour ago," he told the others, "that she's going to get away with it. Anyway, she'll live. The stomach wounds are not all that serious. They can't tell yet what the effect of the head wound will be. I've talked to London over the embassy's direct radio link. There's a private plane coming to take her and her husband to Cyprus. The R.A.F. will get them home from there. A bed's arranged for her in a discreet clinic in Buckinghamshire."

"The Jordanians don't want Mark Dunton?" asked Miller.

"The Jordanians are very happy not to know anything about the affair at all."

After a pause, Chapman said, "You have to admire them. They damn nearly pulled it off."

"They had luck, happening to be on the route the cars were taking," Kennard answered. "Whether they'd have got to them from any distance is doubtful. I suppose they might have, on those bicycles."

"Was it Arafat?"

"I don't know. Maybe. I thought it was at the time, but I wasn't sure."

"To join the peace mission looking like an escort was neat," said Chapman.

"Better than neat. Brilliant. Giles is a loss. We could have used him."

"What about him?" asked Miller.

Kennard shrugged. "Now that the cease-fire is on, trucks are already collecting the corpses from the streets. Later they'll dig them from the houses. All the dead guerrillas are being pitched—with honors, of course—into a huge common grave just outside Wahdat refugee camp."

Curious, Chapman asked, "Won't it be awkward at home? I mean, death certificate and all that. He can't just disappear."

"He hasn't. Giles Dunton died when he fell over a high cliff, on a vacation motoring tour of remote mountains in the north of Lebanon. His brother, who saw the fall, and badly injured his own leg trying to get to him, had him buried locally—the heat, you understand. No doubt there will be a stained-glass window erected in his memory in the village church in Dorset. It's a Dunton family tradition. The Lebanese authorities haven't questioned the facts. We have, naturally, a few particular friends of the department in Lebanon. The death will be properly recorded in London. All the necessary papers will be provided, and will be in order.

"One thing you can always rely on Whitehall for," said Kennard, "is efficient paperwork."

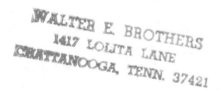